NEVER LEAVE ME

BORIS BACIC

Contents

PROLOGUE

I have terrible taste in men.

Ever since I discovered my attraction toward the opposite sex, I've gotten myself in a ton of trouble just because of the types of men I chose to date. My mother always told me to go for the nice, geeky guy with straight A's because they always made excellent husbands, fathers, and providers.

I don't know if I was unconsciously trying to spite her, but the exact opposite types are the ones I've always felt attracted to. Give me a man with tattooed arms who ditches school to smoke cigarettes while riding his bike, and I'll be swooning over him.

I always knew those kinds of men were accidents waiting to happen, but I just couldn't help wanting to be with them. I couldn't imagine settling down and being a stay-at-home mom or housewife. Back then, my teenage mind thought I'd be dating bad boys and partying forever.

I didn't learn my lesson after my first boyfriend slapped me so hard he busted my lower lip, nor the time my third boyfriend cheated on me with my best friend and then convinced me he loved me, nor the time I had to pepper spray a guy I dated for three months in college because he couldn't take a breakup.

The time when I finally learned my lesson was when I was ready to do so.

My mother always said I went with my head through walls, and she was right. Rather than opt for the beaten path, I walked through bushes and thorns just to make sure I didn't miss anything there.

Then, when I was twenty-four, a guy I had dated for six months beat me to within an inch of my life for accusing him of cheating on me. Another thing I should have seen coming early on, especially because he'd told me he'd hit his ex-girlfriend before, but again, I'm good at ignoring red flags.

The neighbors upstairs had heard the commotion and called the police, and he was locked up. By then, my desire to date bad boys was already waning, and I was leaning more toward everything my mother had been telling me for years.

I still couldn't imagine dating a scrawny, nice guy with thick glasses, though, but I did start to transition toward dating men without a criminal record.

Eventually, the thought of being with a biker who likes to binge drink and sleep in tents during music festivals started to sicken me. I'm twenty-nine now, thirty in a few months, and I feel like I'm running out of time. Pretty soon, finding a suitable candidate for a husband will become a lot more difficult.

Even if I find a boyfriend now, it will take months, maybe even a whole year before he proposes, maybe even longer. Then there's the time we have to spend planning the wedding, and if everything goes according to plan, I'll have just enough time to catch the final train to become a mother.

Maybe I'm getting ahead of myself. I think it's my mother's words influencing me. She's been telling me the same thing for so many years that I've started to believe her.

I don't know how dating will be in my thirties, but I already dread it. With age comes baggage, and that means we need to either tolerate or help resolve insecurities that our future partners carry. It's a mutual rehab process, but it's something I'm not sure how to handle.

In our twenties, we're care-free. If the relationship doesn't work out, who cares? We just go out there and find a new partner.

But once we hit the big three-oh? The pool becomes smaller and more populated with weirdos.

That brings me to today.

I'm at my boyfriend Mark's place. We've been dating for a month now. Mark is very handsome, very polite, a gentleman, and he makes six figures from his jobs as an English teacher and an actor in the theater. You could argue that I've struck gold, but you'd be wrong.

Either I'm still really good at ignoring red flags, or the universe wants to screw with me because, behind closed doors, Mark is nowhere as nice as he presented himself to me on our first date.

In fact, he's such a terrible human being that it makes me wish I had continued dating the bad guys that I was so attracted to.

4 MONTHS EARLIER...

CHAPTER 1

He says his name is Mark.

I see him the moment Catherine and I enter Kayla's apartment. He is standing across the room, alone, grabbing a drink. He looks really good in the white shirt that reveals the muscles on his forearms and jeans that accentuate his ass.

Our eyes briefly meet, and he flashes me a smile full of pearly white teeth. I can feel my cheeks burning up, and I quickly avert my gaze in embarrassment. By the time I look again, he's gone, merged with the crowd filling the room.

I'm about to tell Kayla that I didn't know she knew such hot guys, but she's already gone, too. As the organizer of the party, I assume she has a lot of things to tend to.

Her apartment is pretty spacious, but the crowd makes it look small. The booming music makes it impossible to hear myself speak. I feel the beats inside my ribcage. It's way too hot even though I'm underdressed for this time of the year.

The scent of booze permeates the air. The way the people are laughing and flailing their limbs to the rhythm of the music tells me they're already intoxicated. I feel like I need to do some catching up.

A hand falls on my shoulder, and I turn to see Catherine leaning toward my ear.

"Come on, Amy!" she shouts, and I can still just barely hear her. "Let's get something to drink."

I nod and then shout into her ear, "I'll take care of the drinks. You find us a spot to sit or whatever."

Catherine nods, and we split up. I go toward the table with all the plastic cups and drinks. I'm darting my eyes in various directions, looking for the handsome guy I saw just earlier. He's nowhere in sight, concealed by the dense crowd.

I have to sidle between people to get through the room. It takes me a whole minute of stepping on people's shoes and apologizing before I'm finally at the table, but I then have to wait for a crowd in front of me to clear out.

They take their sweet time filling their cups, and on his way out of there, one of them waves the cup in his hand too violently and his sloshing drink spills on the floor. I hope no one slips on that, but the night is only starting. By morning, I'm assuming Kayla will have a lot of scrubbing to do.

I approach the table and grab two plastic cups. There's a bevy of alcoholic options, but I figure Cat and I should start with something light, so I carefully pour us some beer. I don't even like beer, but hey, nobody drinks alcohol for the taste, right?

I place the bottle back on the table and grab the two cups. I spin around and gasp as I bump into a tall figure standing inches away from me. A bit of beer spills out of my cup but luckily doesn't mess up the person's clothes. The guy has raised his hands defensively, a goofy grin on his face.

"I'm so sorry, I didn't see—" I start to apologize and then realize it's the handsome guy I saw earlier.

I try to suppress my smile, but it's not working. He leans closer and says, "Careful, this is my best shirt."

"I'm sorry," I say again.

12

"Don't worry about it. I'm just joking. I probably should have worn something else. Anything other than white, huh?"

I chuckle but then find that I have no words to keep the conversation going even though I desperately want to. That's the one downside of meeting people at parties. Every second counts. If you don't intrigue someone within the first minute, that's it. Game over.

Not like chatting online where you have time to think of a proper response or when you're on a date in a quiet restaurant and you can actually talk without having to scream at the top of your lungs.

"Two drinks? Won't that be a little too much for you?" he asks.

He's interested in me as much as I'm interested in him, I realize. That's a good start.

"Actually, one is for my friend." I raise one cup.

"Where's your friend now?"

"Should be somewhere in the room. I have no idea, to be honest."

Just then, the song changes to something more upbeat. I hear people cheering at that, and the dancing in the room becomes more vigorous.

The handsome guy leans in again. "Do you think your friend would mind if I borrowed you for one dance?"

My cheeks are burning again. They've been burning for a while now, ever since I bumped into him. I hope I'm not blushing. The lack of proper light in the room should conceal that, I hope.

"Sure." I shrug.

He flashes me another smile. God, he's so gorgeous. He takes the cups from me and places them on the table. He

13

takes my hand and leads me into the crowd. He finds us a spot where we have enough space to dance and reels me in closer.

We start dancing, and I can't help but admire his moves. He doesn't just dance, though. He uses the opportunity to talk to me.

"I'm Mark, by the way," he says.

"Amy," I introduce myself.

"Pretty name."

As the song goes on, Mark and I are gradually inching closer toward each other.

"How do you know Kayla?" he asks.

"We met through a mutual friend. I hadn't talked to her in a while, actually, and then just last week, she invited me to this party to celebrate her new job. What about you?"

"We used to play together a lot as kids. We lived in the same neighborhood, and she used to throw pebbles at my window every morning to get me to come outside. Did you know she was, like, the boss of the entire circle of children in the block?"

"Really?" I ask.

"Yeah. Whatever she decided we would play, we had to listen."

"You were all afraid of a little girl?"

"Hey, she was big and tough back then. Just don't ask her about it because she's really embarrassed about it."

I let out a peal of laughter at that. I imagine Kayla and Mark as kids playing in the street on a sunny summer afternoon. I'm still surprised Kayla has never mentioned Mark. She knows I'm desperate to find a nice boyfriend.

Unless...

14

I try not to think of any nightmarish reasons as to why she wouldn't hook me up with Mark. Speculating is like a rabbit hole, and it can only cause trouble. Then again, I'm sick of dealing with problems only after they arise, and that's why I'm so apprehensive.

Still, Mark's charming smile makes me forget about all my worries, and I'm solely focused on him.

"Who did you come with?" I ask.

"Alone," he says.

"Alone?" I raise my eyebrows.

"Yeah."

"How come?"

Mark shrugs. "I prefer it that way. I don't like to drink too much, and whenever I come with friends, I need to babysit them and drive them home, and it can be a nuisance sometimes. Don't get me wrong, I love going out with them, but sometimes I really need a night for myself, you know?"

I can't say I can relate to it because, my entire life, I've either gone out with friends or boyfriends, never alone. I do like that Mark is peculiar like that, though. It sets him apart from the rest of the guys I've met so far.

Mark and I are talking more than we're dancing until we're just standing and chatting. I don't even know what we're talking about anymore; I just know I'm having fun and I feel very comfortable with him. In fact, I'm enjoying his company so much that I don't even remember that Catherine is waiting for me to return with my drinks until he reminds me.

"Hey, didn't you say you came here with a friend?" he asks.

"Oh, damn," I say. "You're right. I totally forgot."

15

"That's okay. I'm glad I was able to charm you enough into forgetting it." He winks.

"Give me two minutes and I'll be right back," I say.

"I won't be going anywhere."

I rush back to the table with the drinks. The cups I filled are gone, so I fill two more and look for Catherine. Navigating the crowded room with two cups of beer in my hands is pretty difficult, and it's even worse that I don't know where Catherine is.

I eventually find her dancing with a guy. She already has a drink in her hand, and she has her free hand wrapped around the guy's shoulder. He's holding her by the hips, and I can see where this is leading. Looks like she doesn't need me to have fun.

With that, I place the drinks down on the first adequate spot I find and rush back to Mark. My heart flutters in my chest with panic at the thought of not finding him, or worse: Finding him dancing with another woman.

He definitely looks like a player and, let's be honest. Most guys don't go to these kinds of parties to meet the love of their life. They go there because they are looking for one-night stands, right?

I still harbor hope for Mark, though. Maybe he's different. Maybe I'm just too desperate. Either way, it can't hurt to give it a shot.

Well, was I wrong.

Looking back now, if I could travel back in time and change one thing, I never would have returned to that dance stage. I would have bolted out the door and forgotten Mark ever existed.

When I return to the spot where we danced, he's still there, still waiting for me. I don't know why, but I feel like

16

we have a special connection. It's in that moment that I realize that I'm still the same person who's after bad boys because I'm not thinking logically. I'm thinking with my gut.

My inability to say no to my romantic desires got the better of me, and now I'm paying for the consequences.

CHAPTER 2

After dancing until we're sweaty and exhausted, Mark and I find a solitary spot in the apartment and chat while cooling ourselves off with beer.

Okay, maybe I was wrong about the beverage. When you're hot, a cold beer can actually be pretty good. But I'm not focused on the drink. I'm completely absorbed in Mark's eyes and voice.

The corner of the room where we're standing is slightly quieter than the rest of the apartment, so we don't need to shout as loudly as we did back on the dance floor.

"What do you do for a living?" he asks me.

"Just some boring office job," I say.

"Tell me more about it."

I'm flattered that Mark wants to get to know me better, so I indulge him. I work in finances for a corporate company, so I spare him all the irrelevant and boring details. Who would want to listen to someone talking about how they do paperwork all day long anyway?

But surprisingly, Mark is asking me questions about my job, which tells me he's interested in knowing more. He doesn't sound like he's patronizing me, either. The way he's staring at me and nodding tells me he's listening attentively to everything I'm saying, and it makes me so much more attracted to him.

"But enough about me and my boring job. What do you do?" I ask.

"I work as an English teacher, but I also act in the theater part-time," he says.

I almost spit my drink out. "You're an actor?"

"Trust me, it's nowhere near as extravagant as it sounds," he says.

"I hardly believe that. I would love to see you on stage."

"Come to the Rosewood Theater next Friday at eight, and I'll get you a free entrance to the show."

My lips stretch into a wide smile. He doesn't just want a one-night stand. I've dated enough men to know that much.

"I would love that," I say.

"Cool. Wanna dance some more?"

I nod. We go back among the crowd, and this time, we're a lot closer to each other than the first time. As the night goes on, I'm starting to feel the effects of alcohol on me. I start to feel more lively and relaxed.

Before I know it, Mark and I are pressed against each other, his hands on my hips and mine around his shoulders.

It's not sexual like two horny teenagers who can't wait to strip out of their clothes. It's very passionate. We're doing it slowly and sensually, and I feel like I'm melting under the soft caress of his strong hand.

I'm enjoying the moment, and I wish I could freeze it. I can't remember the last time I've been touched like this—in a way that makes me feel both hot and respected at the same time if that makes sense.

I'm expecting our lips to meet, but that doesn't happen even though I want it badly.

When we're done dancing, we return to our spot and talk some more. We're standing so close to each other that I'd practically need to lean just slightly forward and we'd kiss. But I don't do that. We keep talking, and my focus is off because I'm tipsy and because I can't stop thinking about how badly I want him to kiss me.

The night slowly comes to an end. The joviality of the room dies down as people either go home one by one or lose energy from dancing all night long. The music becomes quieter at some point, too. The apartment is empty enough for me to see a bevy of discarded plastic cups on the floor and spilled drinks (and a puddle of vomit).

I can't see Catherine anywhere. She might have gone home with the guy she was dancing with. I probably should have checked up on her, but I had so much fun with Mark that the entire night felt like it lasted no longer than an hour.

The pauses between Mark and me are becoming more frequent, indicating that it's almost time to say goodbye. I'm sleepy, but I want to continue talking to him.

Mark brushes my hair behind my ear and says, "I want to see you again."

That sentence tells me a lot more than it conveys with words. He doesn't want to rush things. He wants to take his time and get to know me because he wants to build something meaningful out of this encounter.

We're on the same page.

"Do you have to go?" I ask just to confirm.

He laughs. "I should have left hours ago, but I couldn't take my eyes off you."

I suppress a schoolgirl-like giggle at that.

"Wanna give me your number?" he asks.

Absolutely, you don't even need to ask.

"Sure." I nod.

He gives me his phone, and I input my number there. He takes his phone back and smiles.

"I look forward to seeing you again," he says. "In the meantime, here's something to remember me by."

He takes a step closer to me and puts a hand on my cheek. I feel my heart rate quickening as his face inches toward mine. When our lips meet, I feel like I'm going to faint.

Wow, what a kiss.

The waiting made it all the more worth it. As our lips brush, I pull him closer to me. We continue kissing for a minute—even though it feels like mere seconds—and then he slowly pulls away. When he does, I feel like I've been hit by a cold wave.

"I'll see you very soon, Amy," he says with a smile.

He turns around, and I watch him as he leaves the apartment. He gives me one final look before closing the door behind him. I pull out my phone and look at the time.

It's almost five a.m. I can't remember the last time I've stayed at a party this long, and I've never stayed up until five to chat with a guy I met. Mark has made me feel weak, and I love that.

I shove the phone into my pocket and start looking for Catherine.

CHAPTER 3

It's noon when I wake up. I'm not hungover, which I'm grateful for.

The same can't be said for Catherine.

I had found her passed out on the couch in Kayla's living room. Since we both had been drinking, driving home had not been an option. I had gotten us an Uber and helped bring Catherine upstairs. She was slurring something about loving me the most of all her friends before I tucked her into bed.

When I returned home, I kicked my clothes off and slipped straight into bed. The excitement from kissing Mark held its clutches on me a while longer before sleep took me.

In the morning, I'm in bed scrolling social media on my phone while I wait to wake up properly. A part of me expected to see a message from Mark when I woke up, but I suppose he's probably still sleeping. He'll call me; I just need to give him some time.

I run into a post by Thomas, an old classmate. He talks about how he's applied to NASA and has a really good feeling about it. I remember that he talked a lot during school about wanting to work for a space company like NASA or SpaceX. In fact, he had talked about it so much that he got the name Astro Thomas.

Most of the kids who wanted to become astronauts or anything like that sort of grew out of it. But not Astro Thomas. He's continued working hard throughout the years, which I've seen on the posts he shares on social media.

I heart react to his post and wish him luck.

When I get fed up with posts that I'm scrolling past, I get out of bed, brush my teeth, take a shower, and put some coffee to brew. I feel like I've slept less than three hours, but at the same time, I don't think I can sleep anymore.

I can already tell this is going to be one of those days where I'm too tired to do anything but not tired enough to get proper rest.

It's the day when I don't feel like watching a movie, but I put it on anyway, and then I stare at the screen like a zombie without actually paying attention. It's the day when I keep glancing at the dirty laundry across the room and tell myself that I need to take care of it, but I don't do it until nightfall, so I leave it for tomorrow.

I don't care, honestly. Last night has left me feeling surprisingly accomplished. I feel like I'm floating on a cloud whenever I think of Mark. I already can't wait to see him again.

I wish I had taken his number like he did mine. This way, he has the entire control over when he's going to text me. I'm okay with him taking the initiative, but not having his number still makes me feel itchy. I tell myself I just have to wait for him to text me.

Meanwhile, the best thing I can do is occupy myself somehow. It might be days before Mark texts me. I can't sit around, waiting by the phone for that to happen. I'm not that much of a loser.

While waiting for coffee to be ready, I make a ham sandwich because I'm starving. Lately, that's my go-to meal whenever I'm too lazy to cook.

I'm trying to be better with cooking discipline, though. My company giving me free meals has made me too lazy in

24

the kitchen. I eat at the office twice a day then order dinner. On the weekends, I rely on delivery services, too.

That's something I'm trying to change step by step.

As I'm standing above the kitchen counter, I'm imagining being a good cook for Mark when we start dating. I blink, caught off guard by that thought. It didn't sound like something I would say, and that scares me.

Then again, is it really so wrong to want to change because of someone you met? My mother would certainly be happy to hear me thinking right now. I have to remind myself that Mark and I aren't dating... yet.

For all I know, he might never even call me. Last night was an entirely different realm. It isn't uncommon for people to wake up and heavily regret doing what they did the night before while alcohol held the reins.

Mark and I didn't do anything big, though. We didn't have sex, in which case I could understand being ghosted—he'd have gotten what he wanted and there would be no need to stay. But that kiss he'd planted on my lips...

Here's something to remember me by.

It was a promise of things to come. He'll call me, I'm sure of that.

I shake my head at the intrusive thoughts that forced their way into my mind once again. This isn't like me—hoping a guy will call me back, I mean. Yes, I can be like that when I fall in love with someone, but I'm not in love with Mark.

"Pull yourself together, Amy," I say to myself as I take the first sip of coffee.

I turn on the TV and let the news anchor talk in the background while I sip coffee and watch videos on TikTok.

The video of a cook preparing ramen noodles is interrupted when someone calls me.

Catherine's name is on top of the screen. I'm surprised she's already awake. She had been so wasted that, when I brought her inside her apartment, I was convinced she wouldn't wake up before three p.m. I swipe to answer the call.

"Hello?" I ask.

"Hey," a croaky voice on the other end says.

"You're up early."

"Ugh." A groan escapes Catherine's mouth. "What happened last night?"

"You can probably guess."

"Are you the one who brought me home?"

"Uh-huh."

There's silence on the line. I use that opportunity to take a sip of coffee.

"There was a guy I danced with," Cat says. "I don't remember what happened next. Have you seen him?"

"I saw you dancing with him, but when it was time to go home, he wasn't there."

"Bummer. He was a real piece of work. I was gonna take him home."

"Yeah, I could see you two getting all handsy."

The sound of something shuffling echoes in the background, and Catherine moans. Then she says, "Hey, you're not so innocent yourself, lady."

"Whatever do you mean?" I play dumb.

"I saw you with that handsome guy in the white shirt. He must have been something if he was able to distract you from coming back with our drinks."

He sure was.

26

"His name's Mark," I say.

"Oh, you even know his name? Look at you, Ms. Serious," Catherine jokes.

Catherine sounds way less croaky now that she's given her vocal cords enough warming up. I'm not sure I like that because it means she'll become a lot more talkative—and tease me about Mark.

"Did you guys... you know?" she asks.

"No. We kissed, though. And I gave him my number," I say.

"Lucky. I should check my phone to see if I have that guy's number memorized."

"Do you even remember what he looks like?"

"Yes. Well, sort of. Hey, he was good enough for me to dance with before I got drunk, so I'll trust last-night-me that he's not faulty."

"Faulty?" I chuckle.

Catherine groans again. "Ugh, my head is killing me. I don't think I'll be ready for work by tomorrow."

I hear popping sounds and something hollow clattering, which I instantly recognize as pills. I hear Catherine gulping twice.

"Don't you have that one big story you're working on due tomorrow?" I ask.

"The one about the corrupt politician? Yeah. God, I hate my job sometimes."

But that's not true. Catherine loves working as a reporter because she gets to invoke the justice she's never seen as a kid. I've never known someone as passionate about their job as her.

"So, tell me about your guy... Mark," she says.

I want to tell Catherine how thrilled I am with Mark and how we spent the entire night talking and dancing, and how I felt when he finally kissed me, but I don't want to reveal how much I like him. If I do and nothing happens, then Catherine is going to start showing pity, and I hate that.

"He's a childhood friend of Kayla's. He works as a teacher and an actor," I say as atonally as I can.

Another gulp on the other side of the phone. "Actor? As in, a movie actor?"

"No, he acts in theaters."

"Dude, that's sick. Imagine how fire the role play is going to be in the bedroom. I should have been the one to get us those drinks."

"Stop." I roll my eyes.

"When are you guys going out?"

"I don't know. I'm waiting for him to call me."

"Why don't you call him instead?"

I hesitate. "I don't have his number."

"Okay," Catherine says, but I can hear what she's trying to communicate with the undertone.

That was really stupid of you, Amy. You should have gotten his number, too. Men are afraid of commitment. They like it when women make the first move.

"He'll call me. He probably just doesn't want to seem too desperate," I say.

"Yeah. Sure," Cat says, and it makes me realize how much I sounded like I'm rationalizing. She quickly adds, "Yeah, I'm sure he will. He looked like he really liked you."

"How do you know? You were drunk."

"I remember seeing the way he looked at you. He was not taking his eyes off you, and I mean, not even for a second."

I smile. I want to ask Catherine if she's messing with me, but I once again don't want to reveal how desperate I am for Mark and me to build something out of the spark we created last night.

"So, are you still going out to that other party tonight?" I ask.

"What? No way. I'm gonna need a few weeks to recover from last night properly. What happened to me? I used to be able to go out drinking on Friday, spend the entire next day awake, drink on Saturday again, and still be ready for another round after twelve hours of sleep. Being in my late twenties sucks."

"It's only going to get worse once we hit our thirties. We don't have the stamina like we used to when we just started out." I shrug.

"Yeah, I guess. Maybe it's time we consider going out to more docile places."

I'm already getting fed up with partying. Just like Catherine, there used to be a time when I didn't miss a single Friday to go out. Then I started doing it every other weekend, and then even less frequently. Nowadays, I go to a party like last night once every few months, and even that seems to drain my energy enough to incapacitate me for the entire following day.

I blame the years of accumulated sleepless nights.

The conversation with Catherine takes a turn there and we talk about other things unrelated to parties and the guys we met. When the conversation ends, I'm feeling a little more energized. It's like a sugar rush, though, and it doesn't last long.

Even coffee doesn't help me with that, so I go to bed in hopes of being able to take a nap. My eyelids are heavy, but sleep refuses to come. Every now and again, I check my phone, only to see zero notifications. As much as I hate to admit it, I'm impatient about receiving a message or a call from Mark.

The day passes slowly and in a blur.

The following day, I'm a lot more productive. I clean the entire apartment, cook food, and even go for a run in the park. It's a nice day out, and I'm basking in the pleasant heat of the sun. There's just one nagging thought that won't let me take a break.

Whenever I look at my phone, I feel a jab of something unpleasant because I haven't received anything from Mark. It worsens when Monday comes and there's still no notification from him.

At work, I greet the tiny cactus on my desk, give it water, and check my phone a lot more often than usual. The image of Mark kissing me forces itself into my mind a lot, too. I can't get that smile and voice out of my head.

Here's something to remember me by.

I start to wonder whether I've given him the wrong number. I want to call Kayla and ask her about Mark, but if I get his number and contact him, he'll know I went out of my way to do it, and I'll seem desperate.

Maybe he's just not interested in me anymore.

When work is done, I pick up my things and go home. It's been a particularly stressful day, so I'm glad it's over. Just when I'm about to take a long, hot shower, I receive a

30

message. I don't think when I open it. In fact, I'm half-expecting it's work.

Except it's not.

Hey, beautiful. How are you?

Mark

My day is immediately a hundred times better.

CHAPTER 4

I won't bore you with details of our first date.

To summarize, Mark and I chatted via text for a little bit before he asked me out. I said yes, of course, but I made it sound in the message like I wasn't too eager. I don't know what the deal is with men, but they really love it when a girl plays hard to get. The more you run toward them, the more they seem to retreat, and the less you're interested, the more they chase you.

It's paradoxical.

I haven't gotten that impression from Mark, but better to be safe than sorry. He invited me out to an Italian restaurant, which might be a little too fancy for my taste, but I get that he was trying to make a good impression.

Seeing Mark in person again makes the butterflies in my stomach go wild. He's even more handsome than I remember.

I'm happy I get to see him away from the flashy lights and the crowds that constantly danced in my peripheral vision. The two of us now have time for ourselves.

I'm not sure how to react when I see him, so I say hi and stop in front of him. He greets me back and then kisses me. I wasn't sure if he wanted to go for a kiss right away, but I'm glad he did. I feel a pleasant surge coursing all the way to my toes when our lips meet, and I realize how much I've yearned for this.

I don't even care about the restaurant anymore. I just want to kiss him all night long.

Mark is the one who puts the brakes on things and suggests we go inside. The conversation at the table is slow at first. I'm guessing we're both nervous even though Mark doesn't look like it.

The problem is I don't know how exactly to behave. Do I act reserved like this is the first time we've met? Do I flirt with him? Do I act like we're already dating?

I decide to let him take the lead. I love a man who can do that, and Mark is obviously capable of it.

As the date goes on and we order food, the conversation between us starts to flow more naturally, just like that night when we first met. I realize just how relaxed I was at the party compared to how I am now.

When you're at a crowded party, you don't have any expectations. You don't think you'll ever see the same people again, so you're yourself more. But on a date where it's only you and the other person? The stakes are higher. Both of you are invested, at least a little bit, so naturally, you're more nervous.

Dinner comes to an end, and I don't even remember what Mark and I have been talking about. I just know I've had a wonderful time and I couldn't stop observing him with scrupulous detail.

When we're out of the restaurant, we're kissing again. He's a lot more touchy this time, and I have to say I'm enjoying it. We're both out of breath when our lips pull apart. My mouth hurts from how long we've been kissing, and I love that sensation.

"I know this may be early, but do you wanna go back to my place?" he asks.

I'm not stupid. I know what that means. My brain keeps screaming at me to slow things down, but I don't listen to it. It's too quiet against the loud desires of my body. I nod, and Mark leads us to the parking lot where he parked his car.

We can hardly get our hands off each other on the drive to his apartment. When we arrive, I don't even have a proper chance to get a look at his place because we're undressing and kissing the whole time. We spend the entire night in his bedroom. I don't even know when I fall asleep. I think I just pass out from exhaustion.

When I next open my eyes, the sun is peering through the blinds. I think the bright rays are what woke me up. I'm lying on Mark's shoulder, enjoying the warmth of his body and the way his chest rises and falls with each breath.

I can't stop looking at him and running my finger down his cheek. He's gorgeous even when he's asleep, and the bedraggled hair somehow adds to it. I hate separating from him, but I have to roll over to reach for my phone on the nightstand.

I unlock it and my eyes widen.

"Oh, shit," I say as I quickly throw the heavy blanket off and stand.

That wakes Mark up. He raises his head and asks, "What's going on?"

"I'm late for work," I say as I slip into my bra and panties.

Mark rubs his eyes, squints against the light penetrating the room, then props himself on his elbows. "Sorry. It's my fault."

"No, what are you talking about?" I ask.

"I didn't even ask you if you had work today." Mark yanks the blanket off and stands up.

I love how considerate he is. If I had a second, I would have stopped dressing just to cross the room and kiss him.

You know what? I can spare that second, so that's exactly what I do. He smiles at that.

"You're too sweet," I say.

"Are they gonna give you trouble at work?" he asks.

"No. Don't worry about it, cutie." I pinch his cheek.

I'm just so overwhelmed with the emotions I'm feeling toward him that I don't know how to express them, and it comes out in the form of a pet name and a pinch.

"Let me at least give you a ride, then," he says.

"It's fine. I'll grab an Uber. You can go back to bed."

I've stopped dressing again, and I'm hugging Mark. I don't care if I lose a few more minutes. I'm already late, so I might as well absorb Mark as much as possible before I need to leave.

"Please. I insist," he says.

When he puts it that way, I can't say no.

On the drive there, I quickly fix my hair as much as I can and put makeup on. It doesn't look as great as it normally would, but it'll have to do. I'll figure something out during lunchtime.

When Mark drops me off at the office, I spend an entire minute saying goodbye to him. By saying goodbye, I really mean kissing him until my lipstick is ruined again, and I end up using wet wipes to get it off my face entirely.

"See you tonight?" Mark asks.

I nod, not even stopping to consider whether I have any plans. I'm sure that, even if I have something, I can push it to another time.

I don't get any weird looks at the office, which I'm grateful for. The first thing I do is greet the tiny cactus on

36

my desk. It's become sort of a habit, but I only talk to it when I'm sure no one can hear me.

The day goes by very slowly because I hardly got any sleep, and my head is too wrapped up around the night I spent with Mark. By noon, I have my third coffee and gently slap myself to focus on the work at hand. Since I work in finances, I can't afford to make any mistakes.

The email I receive from Mark sobers me up.

Hey, beautiful. Working hard? :)
Mark

I don't know how he got a hold of my work email, but I imagine it's not terribly difficult to do that. I'm also not happy he's emailing me on my company laptop. Don't get me wrong, I miss him, but I can't go acting like a teenager while I'm at work, so I send him a brusque reply.

Missing me so much already? I feel the same way. I can't talk from this email because I can get in trouble, but I'll be sure to call you as soon as I'm free.

I send a kissing smiley face at the end of the message.

My assumption is that he gets the hint because he doesn't reply.

I can't describe how happy I am to be out of the office at five p.m. sharp. As soon as I'm home, I fall headlong into bed without even taking my clothes off and fall asleep. I'm woken up by a call from Mark. It's already dark out by then, and I curse myself for sleeping for that long afternoon because now I'll have trouble falling asleep during bedtime.

Mark wants to take me out to the aquapark, and I don't say no. I have a few hours to get ready, so I do so, and by the time he picks me up, I'm feeling fresh and ready to spend another whole night with him if necessary.

We spend more time looking at each other than the fish in the water tanks. It's not about what you do at places like those anyway. It's about who you do them with.

When we're done, he drops me off at home. I invite him inside, and he accepts the invitation. We don't spend the entire night being naughty, though. He leaves close to midnight, saying that he has work.

"Thanks for inviting me in, babe," he says.

Babe.

Hearing him call me that stirs something pleasant in my chest. That's how I know we are now officially dating.

That's how the problems in my life start.

CHAPTER 5

Mark and I spend every day together. Outside of work, we're pretty much inseparable.

I feel as though things might be going a little too fast. Not even a week later, he says three big words that catch me off guard.

We're lying in bed at his place, joking and laughing, when he says, "I love you."

The buoyant atmosphere in the room drops like an anchor. I'm so caught off guard that I go mute. Mark is staring at me expectantly, waiting for me to say it back. I can feel the temperature of the room dropping with each passing second. If I don't do something soon, the romantic moment will turn into something awkward and terrible.

I don't think things through when I tell him, "I love you too."

I'm not completely sure if it's the right thing to say. I don't even know if I feel it. It's been a week since we started dating, and things seem to be moving in the right direction, but I still consider saying those three words a step that should not be taken lightly.

So, why did I tell Mark I love him even though I'm not sure if I actually feel that?

Well, first of all, because it's really awkward when someone tells you they love you and you don't say it back. Secondly, I'm kind of bad at recognizing my own emotions. I don't know what I feel until much later. For all I know, I do love Mark; I just have all my emotions jumbled up right now and it's hard for love itself to surface above everything else.

The moment I tell Mark I love him, too, the smile on his face stops dropping. He kisses me harder and holds me against his chest. That's the first time I feel a pang of discomfort. Not physically but inside my chest.

While we're lying there, I'm rethinking whether I made the mistake by telling him the L word. I'm trying to find a way to retract it without it sounding awkward, but I mean, come on, how does a person even do that?

I figure that lingering on it will only cause more damage, so I settle for the fact (hope) that, even if I don't love him now, I'll start to soon, and there will be no need to take anything back.

"I'm gonna take a shower," he says. "Wanna join?"

"In a bit," I say.

When he stands, I grab my phone. I scroll stories on Instagram and run into one by Astro Thomas. It's a picture of his acceptance letter from NASA with his caption above "I'M IN!"

I can't help but smile. I feel happy for him. His hard work has paid off, and he's shown that anything is possible if you never give up. I send him a bunch of hearts to show how happy I am for him.

When I look up, Mark is still standing there, staring at me with a deadpan look.

"What?" I ask.

He smiles, but it looks anything but genuine. "Nothing."

He then disappears into the bathroom.

Three days later is when the first problems in our relationship start.

We're at the movies, and I tell Mark I'm going to buy some popcorn. He nods and waits by a table since we still have time before the movie starts. When I get to the popcorn counter, I see a familiar face behind it.

"Travis!" I call out to my former high school classmate.

"Hey, Amy. Didn't think you were still living here, to be honest," he says.

"Yeah. I got lucky with the job I landed, so... here I am."

"Cool." He nods.

"And look at you. You also seem to be doing good."

I'm not being sarcastic. Travis had dropped out of high school after his parents got divorced. He had a pretty tough life, and I heard that he even got arrested at one point. Considering all of that, working as the popcorn guy is a pretty good turnaround.

"I am. I'm working toward getting my GED, and I hope to get a better job after that," he says.

"That's great to hear. I'm really happy for you." I smile.

"Thanks. What can I get for you?"

I choose the popcorn, and I pay him. He gives it to me, and I wish him luck with his education and job hunting before returning to Mark.

Except, when I get back to him, I can tell something is terribly wrong. He's not smiling like he did before I left. His face is drooping as if he's just been told that his mother died.

"What's wrong, baby?" I ask.

"Nothing," he coldly retorts. "Let's go. The movie is about to start."

He stands and strides across the hallway without even taking my hand or looking at me. He's so obviously cold, and I'm too afraid to ask him what's up because he looks like he might start yelling at me.

We watch the movie in silence. He doesn't look at me or touch me once during the two hours. I can hardly focus on the screen. All I can think about is whether Mark is angry at me and why. What could have happened during those five minutes while I was gone getting popcorn from—

Oh, no.

I think I get it. Or, do I? As soon as the idea enters my mind, I dismiss it because it's so ridiculous. I glance in Mark's direction and see his face illuminated by the flashing screen. He's staring ahead but looks like he's bored.

I lean closer to him. "Wanna grab dinner after this?"

I'm trying to gauge whether he's really angry or if I'm imagining things.

"Not really. I should head home. Got work tomorrow," he says atonally.

Okay, he's definitely angry, but I still don't know why.

When the movie is done and we're out in the street, I carefully observe him. He hasn't looked at me once, and he hasn't said a word.

"Mark?" I ask.

"What?" he asks.

He's still looking elsewhere.

"Why won't you look at me?" I ask.

That's when our eyes finally meet. I can see a change in that gaze. It's no longer sparkling with affection. It's full of animosity that I didn't even know Mark was capable of feeling toward me.

It doesn't just make me uncomfortable. It scares me because it helps me realize just how little I know this man. We've known each other for just under a week, and that

42

isn't nearly enough time to see even the tip of the iceberg that is someone's flaws.

Now that we're getting comfortable around each other, those flaws are starting to peek between the cracks, and I realize just how much we've been rushing things.

Mark's lips stiffen into a thin line, and his nostrils expand. He wants to say something, and it looks as if he's trying his best not to hurl the most devastating insult in my direction.

"Did I do something?" I ask.

Mark's mouth pulls back into a smile, but it's one of those smiles that you make when you're frustrated or in utter disbelief.

"I saw you flirting with the popcorn guy back there," Mark says.

I cannot believe his words, and yet, they don't come as a surprise. My mouth drops and I can't form a single word, except, "What?"

"Yeah, don't think I didn't catch you smiling and giggling with him. And right in front of me, too."

"What?" I ask again with a shake of my head.

"First he butters your popcorn, then he butters something else, right?"

"What?!" I raise my tone this time.

Mark's final sentence is so ridiculous that I can't tell if he's serious or not. I want to burst out laughing, but I can see he's dead serious, so I refrain from doing so. This is obviously no laughing matter.

At least, not to him.

"I don't know if you're aware of this, Amy, but when two people are in a relationship, they're supposed to be loyal to each other," Mark says.

43

Some passersby are turning their heads in our direction, and I'm starting to feel embarrassed.

"Can we talk about this in the car, please?" I ask.

"No. We're going to talk about it right now," he says.

I cross my arms. "Fine. The popcorn guy is my high school classmate."

I expect the realization of how much he messed up to wash over his face. That doesn't happen. If anything, he remains firm in his stance.

"So?" he asks.

"Mark, are you serious?" I spread my arms quizzically.

"Do I look like I'm joking?"

It's like I'm speaking to an entirely different person. Who is this hostile man, and why is he attacking me like this? He's nothing like the gentle, caring boyfriend that's taking care of me like I'm a flower with vulnerable petals.

"I can't believe you right now," I say.

"I demand an explanation, Amy. Why were you flirting with the popcorn guy?"

"I wasn't flirting with him! We were just catching up because we haven't seen each other since high school!"

No idea why I'm justifying my actions to him. I didn't do anything wrong. All I did was buy popcorn and have a minute-long small talk with a guy I went to school with for two years. Mark is making me feel like I've cheated on him, and I'm not that kind of a person.

"Well, it sure looked like you were swooning over him," Mark says.

"We were *talking*. What part of that don't you understand?" I ask.

I feel like I'm talking to a wall. Is Mark even listening to me, or is he too enthralled in his jealousy to hear my side of the story?

This is all getting ridiculous. I don't want to have this discussion anymore. And yet, Mark's outlandish statements are somehow luring me like a magnet back into the argument, forcing me to defend myself even though I did nothing wrong.

Or did I?

I quickly replay in my head whether I could have possibly said something to Travis that might have alluded to flirting. No, of course I didn't. When I'm dating someone, I only have eyes for that person and no one else. If I did say something inappropriate, then it wasn't with the intention of it sounding so.

But I didn't say anything, did I?

I'm sure I didn't. Mark is just gaslighting me into thinking I did. That realization makes me resentful toward him. I'm very disappointed that we're even having this discussion. I know we don't know each other, but does he think I'm such a slut that I would flirt right in front of him not even a week into our relationship?

Mark is saying something accusatory again, but I'm not listening. I raise my hand and interrupt him.

"You know what? I refuse to have this discussion," I say as calmly as I can, but I sure don't feel like it. "I'll see you when you've calmed down. Have a good day, Mark."

I turn to leave, ignoring Mark calling out to me. More and more heads are turning in our direction, now with concern rather than curiosity. If this continues, someone is bound to call the cops, and that's not the kind of attention I want.

"Hey! Hey, wait! Where are you going?" Mark calls out behind me, and I can hear he's not at my heels anymore. "Where are you going?"

I don't respond. As soon as I round the corner, I pick up my pace. Only when I'm on the other side of the street do I turn around to make sure Mark isn't following me.

He's nowhere in sight, and I'm unsure if I should feel glad or disappointed. Part of me had hoped he'd come running after me to apologize for being such a jerk. Then again, even if he did that, I'd still be angry, so maybe it's best if we cool off for now.

Right there is when I should have ended the relationship with Mark, but I didn't. You might think I'm crazy, but I've been in so many abusive relationships that I'm having trouble telling where the line should be drawn.

No, the relationship with Mark is far from over, and at moments, I will wish I was dead.

CHAPTER 6

My phone vibrates on the bus ride home, but I don't check it. I know the messages are from Mark, and I refuse to get into a discussion with him before I've cooled off.

When I enter the apartment, I can no longer take the suspense, so I unlock my phone. As expected, the messages are from him. I also have two missed calls.

Babe, I'm sorry, okay?

I overreacted, and I'm really sorry. Please pick up your phone.

I don't answer him right away. I may be petty, but I want him to simmer in anticipation. I want him to suffer for making me suffer with his jealous outburst. I put my phone on do not disturb, set it down, and go into the bathroom to take a shower.

I take my time with it, and after that, I do some chores around the house. I'm hoping Mark is eaten away by guilt during this time but, the truth of the matter is that I, too, am feeling terrible. Me spiting him is hurting me as much as it's hurting him—maybe even more.

Eventually, I can't take it anymore so I retrieve my phone and see a couple more missed calls and messages from him. I take a moment to compose myself. I'm completely calm, but I don't know how I should behave on the call.

Do I act as cold as he was in the movies? Is that only going to make things worse?

You know what? I'll let him take the lead and see how things go from there. I'm no longer angry over his jealous fit, but if he doubles down on what he said before, I might get angry again.

I dial Mark's number and raise the phone to my ear. He answers before the first ring ends.

"Hello? Amy?" he asks.

He sounds agitated.

"Hi," I say and offer nothing else.

"Hey," he says back. A moment of awkward silence stretches between us before he speaks up again. "Thank you for calling me back, babe. I was worried about you."

"Mhm."

"Listen, I'm sorry. I overreacted, okay? I'm sorry. I just..." He sighs into the phone. "I didn't mean it to sound like that, I promise. I just..."

He's having difficulty forming sentences, but I don't say anything into the phone, not even a sound that would let him know I'm still here and listening to him. I don't care if it makes him feel uncomfortable.

"I'm doing my best not to get jealous like this," he says. "It's just hard sometimes because of my past relationship."

That breaks my stalwart stance a little.

"I didn't tell you about this, but I had a relationship for over five years," he says. "We broke things off about two years ago. I haven't gotten into anything serious since then. I couldn't because I needed time to fix all the damage she inflicted on me. I still have some repairs to do, you know?"

I gulp. "What happened?"

"A lot of things," he says. "She cheated on me with multiple partners for years. I only found out when she admitted that it was getting serious with one of them and was dumping me. It was, uh..."

He pauses then lets out a chuckle and sniffles. Is he crying?

"It's okay if you can't talk about it," I say.

I'm suddenly feeling sympathetic toward him. How hadn't I realized it before? The extreme reaction to me flirting with the popcorn guy wasn't him being a psycho. It was sensitivity to past trauma.

"No, it's fine," he says. "She dumped me for a coworker she told me I have nothing to worry about."

"Mark, I'm so sorry," I say.

I want to hug Mark tightly until he's feeling okay again and tell him I won't do the same thing to him. Not only am I feeling a surge of sympathy toward him, but I can also sense a wave of anger toward his ex.

Who would do such a thing to another human being? If you don't love your partner enough to stay loyal, then you should at least not be a coward and break things off with them before you go looking for other people.

I don't know who Mark's ex is, but I want to slap her and call her a bitch.

"It was just a roller coaster with her, you know?" Mark says. "I never knew where we stood, and she always made me feel like I wasn't good enough, no matter what I did. It really ruined my self-esteem, and I'm only now starting to build it back up to where it was before I met her."

"I'm so sorry, baby," I say. "I didn't know."

"It's fine. I'm the one who should be apologizing. I overreacted. It's just... when I saw you laughing with that guy, it triggered something inside me. It was like I was going through the same stuff all over again."

"Baby... Are you home right now?"

"Yeah."

"Hold on. I'll be there soon."

There's a slight pause. "Really?"

"Yes. I want to be there with you. To show you how important you are to me."

He lets out a chuckle. "Okay. Thank you, Amy."

"Don't thank me for that."

"Okay."

"I'll be there in twenty minutes."

I hear Mark sucking in a breath of air. There's reluctance in his voice, and then he says, "I love you."

"I love you, too," I say.

It doesn't matter how I feel right now. Mark needs to hear those words, and I'm not going to deprive him of it.

If only I knew it was all a part of his plan.

CHAPTER 7

Everything goes okay for the next few days.

I go to the theater on Saturday to watch Mark's performance. He is extremely talented. When I'm watching him up on that stage, it's like I'm watching an entirely different man. He's taken on the persona of a traveling merchant, and he's playing it in such a convincing manner that I'm sitting at the edge of my seat with bated breath.

I feel so much more attracted to him now that I see his impressive acting skills. I also have to admit that I like the fact that he's opened up to me about his weaknesses from his past relationship. Many girls would find those vulnerabilities unattractive, but to me, they're sexy because Mark trusts me enough to share his insecurities with me, which means he believes I can fix him.

There's nothing more empowering to a woman's ego than that.

I've already forgotten about the fight Mark and I had at the movies. It seems like such a minor thing that I don't give it a second thought. Not until our next fight anyway. I'll get to that later.

I'm pretty much ready to announce to the world that I have a boyfriend, so Mark and I officially post on Facebook that we're dating. If it's not on Facebook, then it didn't happen, right?

Catherine calls me right away so the two of us can scream into each other's ears with happiness. I tell her all the details and, after ten minutes, I feel like we've been talking only about me the entire time, so I ask her what's new on her end.

"Well, I kind of started dating the guy from the party I danced with. His name's Rick," she says.

There's more happy screaming while she tells me details about Rick.

I don't find it surprising that I haven't seen Catherine posting anything about her relationship online. She's a reporter, and she likes to stay under the radar with everything.

For a while, I feel happy with Mark. I was happy before as well, but having Mark in my life is like discovering a piece of a puzzle I never knew was missing. Unfortunately, as time goes by, I start to discover that the high I've been feeling was just that—a high.

I'm no longer in the phase where I'm so crazy about Mark that I have to see him every day. I still can't tell whether I love him, but I do like him, and I'm hoping that the emotion will soon transmogrify into love.

Anyway, it's way too late to take it back now. Mark already suffers from low self-esteem issues, so me telling him that I never loved him these past few weeks even though I said otherwise would break his trust again.

As time goes on, the one thing that's starting to bother me, however, is how needy Mark is. I don't even realize that's what's been bothering me until I'm at work one day, feeling crappy because I'm tired and dealing with annoying coworkers, and I get a message from Mark.

Hey, babe, what are you up to? Just wanted to let you know that I'm thinking about you and to ask if you wanna go to the park today.

The message is supposed to bring a smile to my face, but all it does is make me want to chuck my phone across the room. I force myself to calm down, telling myself that I'm just frustrated because of work.

But as I stare at the message, I realize that, no, that's not the reason. I've been feeling like this for a few days now, and it's because, on top of answering calls and emails eight hours a day at the office, I also have to answer texts and calls outside of it—and most of them are from Mark.

I loved the attention at first because it made me feel how much Mark cared. Now that the emotions have settled, I want to have some alone time from time to time, and it's difficult with him constantly calling, messaging, or asking to meet up.

I don't want to tell him that, though. He means no harm. So instead, I leave my phone on silent and decide to respond when I feel like it. I then get back to work and, I have to say, not hearing the constant vibrations from notifications is refreshing.

It's not just Mark, though. The fact that we're so closely connected to the rest of the world with numerous social media apps on our phones makes it impossible to stay focused for longer than a few minutes before getting interrupted.

Researchers say that our attention span dropped by over twenty-five percent in just the past few years. I can feel it affecting my productivity and sleep, and I hate it. Even as I'm working with my phone on silent, I have the urge to pick it up and check it out, even though there's no reason for me to do so.

I get a lot of work done by lunch time, and I feel happy with myself. I should stop bringing my phone to my desk altogether because I can wrap things up so much faster. I wish I could say that I can finish work and go home earlier, but if I do that too often, management will realize they can shove more work in my direction, and I don't want that.

I go to the cafeteria and grab lunch. I put my platter down at an unoccupied table, pull my phone out to entertain myself while I'm eating, and I'm ready to take the first bite of the sizeable burrito when my manager Cindy comes along.

"Hey, Amy? I'm going to need that report we talked about by the end of the day," she says.

"I already sent it to you," I say.

Truthfully, I'm annoyed that she's interrupting my lunch break to talk about work. While I'm on my break, I'm not an employee. I'm a person eating lunch and doing literally anything that's not work.

Cindy frowns. "I haven't received anything."

"Really? I must have forgotten to hit send. I'll do it once I'm back at my desk."

In other words, please leave me alone. I don't dislike my manager. Quite the contrary. She's very nice and friendly, and I feel like I can voice my work concerns to her whenever I have any. For me, lunch break is a sanctity, and I refuse to desecrate it by talking about work.

"Okay. Oh, and I need you to email the client and ask him if we can extend the deadline by two days," Cindy says.

I nod, swiping a finger across the screen of my phone to unlock it. "Sure, I'll do it right after—"

The sentence dies in my throat when my eyes fall on the screen.

"You okay?" Cindy asks.

I snap my head away from the screen and force a nod. I can hardly focus on my conversation with Cindy. "Uh, yeah. I, um... I'll do what you asked after lunch."

"All right. Thanks, Amy."

Cindy leaves, thank God. I turn my attention back to the screen and stare at the million notifications from Mark.

"What the hell," I utter under my breath.

I have twelve missed calls and seven messages. I read through the messages, and each is more frenetic than the last one. After asking me if I wanted to go to the park, Mark sent:

Babe, are you there?
Hello?
Why aren't you picking up?
Pick up.
For Christ's sake, Amy, pick up your phone.
Call me.
Why are you ignoring me?

He and I already spoke this morning while I was on my way to work. Only a few hours have passed since then, and he's already panicking like I'm dead or something.

"Amy?" a timid voice calls to me from the cafeteria's entrance.

I snap my head up. It's the receptionist, Emily. She has a worried look on her face. What the hell is going on today?

Pushing the chair back, I stand, put my phone into my pocket, leaving the savory burrito untouched, and stride over to Emily.

"What's up?" I ask against the lump formed in my throat.

"Come with me, please," Emily says.

She looks very uncomfortable. I don't like where this is going.

I follow Emily out into the hallway where she stops to face me. She puts her hands together and says, "I just got off the phone with someone asking about you."

I gulp. I already know who it was. Still, I ask anyway.

"Wh-who was it?" I don't mean to stutter, but I can't control it.

"He introduced himself as Mark and said he's a friend of yours."

"Okay. And, what did he want?"

"He said you weren't answering his calls, and he was worried something might have happened to you, so he wanted us to check up on you."

What the hell?

"I see." I swipe my hand across my forehead. My fingers come off wet from the cold beads of sweat that have broken out on my skin. "Well, I'm okay. I'll let him know. Sorry for the hassle, Emily."

I nod and turn to leave, but Emily calls out to me, stopping me in my tracks. I knew there'd be trouble from this. Great. Not gonna get off the hook so easily.

"What is it?" I ask.

"The higher-ups know about the call, and they're not happy that someone is not only disturbing you during work but also calling the company to cause issues because of an employee's personal problems. We understand that personal problems are unavoidable, but bringing them into work is not acceptable."

Emily sounds like she's a walking company manual quoting a section word by word.

"Am I in trouble?" I ask because the suspense is killing me.

I just want to know if I should pack my things and start looking for a new job.

"No. You're fine this time. But please make sure it doesn't happen again," Emily says.

"Yes, of course. It won't. Thank you, Emily."

Emily flashes me a PR smile. "You have a great day now."

It's the fakest smile I've ever seen, one that she needs to execute hundreds of times in a single day whenever important people walk past the reception. I'm too busy feeling relieved to be bothered by Emily.

My palms are clammy, and I feel like I've just dodged a bullet that flew right next to my ear.

I'm supposed to return to the cafeteria and eat my lunch, but I no longer have an appetite. If I take just a bite of that burrito, I'm going to vomit.

Instead, I rush inside the bathroom on the fourth floor (that one is almost never used, and it's going to give me enough privacy), close myself inside one of the stalls, and dial Mark's number.

He picks up on the first ring.

"Oh, thank God, you're okay," he says.

"What the hell were you thinking, Mark?" I ask.

I wasn't going to start the conversation that way, but I can't help it. I'm way too angry to control myself.

Mark doesn't speak, so I use that chance to continue berating him. "Do you know how much trouble you got me into because of what you did?"

"Babe..." he starts.

"Have you even stopped to consider that I'm busy working? Seriously!"

"Amy, you weren't answering my calls or messages. What did you expect me to do?"

"I was *working*!" I hiss.

"Oh yeah? Well, how do I know that?"

"Excuse me?"

"You haven't answered my messages in hours. What am I supposed to think?"

I use my free hand to rub my nose bridge.

"I was at work. I was busy," I emphasize every word as if I'm speaking to a child.

How and when did my intention to scold him turn into me defending myself... again?

"For all I know, you could be out with someone else right now," Mark says.

I pause to try to figure out whether Mark is joking.

"You're joking, right? Please tell me you're joking," I say.

"I'm sorry for sounding like a jerk, but you haven't given me a reason to trust you," Mark says.

"What is that supposed to mean?" I ask.

I can't believe what I'm hearing. He's acting just like when he accused me of flirting with Travis.

"A few days ago, I saw you smiling at your phone. So when you were in the bathroom, I checked your phone, and I had something to see."

I don't say anything. What can I possibly say? What is he even talking about?

"I saw that you responded to some guy's story on Instagram with a heart, and he replied to you with a kissing smiley face," Mark says.

I'm still at a loss for words. I feel like we're back at the movies and talking about me flirting with Travis. Still, I feel the need to justify myself, so I do just that even though I shouldn't.

"It's a *friend*," I say, putting accent on the last word.

"That's the problem, Amy. You and I don't see eye to eye on that. You never told me you had guy friends. You think it's perfectly fine to have guys as friends. If I knew that, I would have approached this whole thing differently."

Once again, I'm hit with a jab of disbelief. He did not just say that, did he?

"What?" That's all I can manage.

"Men and women can't be friends, Amy."

"You're friends with Kayla," I point out.

Why am I even getting into this discussion? I should just hang up. Something is stopping me from doing so. Stubbornness? The fact that I don't want to leave things between Mark and myself on such bad terms, all because of a misunderstanding?

"Not anymore," he says. "I blocked her ever since you and I started dating."

"You what?"

"Yeah. You're more important to me than her. I don't want her to get in the way of our happiness. And I expect you to do the same for me."

He blocked a friend he's known all his life for a girl he's been dating for a few weeks. Whenever I blink, I see an army of red flags gyrating in front of my face. How have I not seen this before? This man is crazy.

"You're frigging insane," I say, and then hang up.

Before I can do anything else, my phone starts ringing. I decline Mark's call and turn off my phone.

He's already ruined lunch for me. I am not going to let him distract me from work.

CHAPTER 8

I'm hardly able to focus on work today. I do everything Cindy asked me to, and as soon as the clock ticks five, I'm out of there.

My mind is still stuck on the conversation with Mark.

He snooped around my phone because he didn't trust me.

He accused me of fooling around while I was at work.

He blamed me for having guy friends.

What the actual hell?

My blood is boiling even when I leave the office. I try my best to smile at my coworkers on my way out, especially since the entire office probably already knows that Mark called to check up on me. I doubt I'm successful, but I don't care right now.

I just want to get home and find a way to blow off some steam. On my way home, I keep thinking about where Mark and I stand. Are we still even together?

Well, I didn't break up with him, but maybe Mark will see it that way. No, he's not the kind of guy to let things go easily. He probably doesn't even know what he did wrong.

Honestly, I'm confused at this point. I'm not even sure if I want to be with Mark anymore. The way it all started with him was fiery and intense, and I loved every moment of it. But that spark died so fast and suddenly, as if a strong gust blew in and extinguished it.

That spark is still alive on Mark's end, and that makes things so much harder. If only he felt the same way as me.

But do I really want to break up with him? Is that the right choice to make?

Yes, there are aspects of this relationship that I don't enjoy, but then there are things that I love. Mark is very thoughtful and sweet (when he's not a jerk like today), and he goes above and beyond to make me happy, and our sex is amazing.

Plus, these outbursts are only occasional. They're intense when they happen, yes, but they're occasional. It's because of his ex. He doesn't want to do these things, but his insecurities get the better of him.

I promised him I wouldn't be like her. I promised I'd help him overcome those insecurities. Once that happens, we'll have no more problems. The neediness will disappear, and so will the jealousy.

I step out of the bus and make my way down the street. I'm staring down, deep in my thoughts, and I don't see the person walking in my direction until I bump into her. I gasp and apologize until I realize that I know the person.

"Kayla!" I exclaim.

"Amy. You're walking like a zombie," she says jokingly.

I laugh. "Uh-huh."

"I haven't seen you since the party. How are you?"

"I'm good. Just got out of work."

I hope my lack of response will help her take the hint and let me go. She doesn't.

"Oh, by the way, I saw on Facebook that you have a new boyfriend. Congrats! I'm so happy for you!"

I bite my lip. I don't have the heart to tell Kayla that things aren't going too great between me and Mark.

"Thank you," I say instead.

"So, where'd you guys meet? What's he like? We should meet up one of these days so you can tell me all about him."

"What do you mean? We met at your party."

Kayla's smile is fixed on her face, but her eyes show confusion. "You... did?"

"Yeah. I mean, he's your childhood friend."

The smile now disappears off Kayla's face. "Uh, what?"

That's when I realize just how wrong something is in this entire story.

"Kayla, do you even know who my boyfriend is?" I ask.

"Well, I know his name is Mark, but why would you think he's my friend?"

"Because he told me so. Wait, wait, wait." I put my fingers on my temples to stave off an impending headache. "He was at *your* party. Are you saying he came there uninvited? How did he get in?"

"I don't know, Amy. It was a big party. I saw a lot of people I didn't know, but those all came with someone I know. Maybe he just came with one of them."

"No, he specifically told me he came alone. He also told me you guys used to play together as kids all the time."

Kayla's face is still blasé.

"He went into details when he told me those stories!" I keep pushing.

Kayla shakes her head.

"He said you used to be the boss in the neighborhood! That all the kids played whatever you decided you'd play!" I'm nearly hysterical at this point.

"There were never any kids in the neighborhood where I lived as a kid," she says.

"You must have just forgotten. What, are you trying to tell me some stranger snuck into your apartment, and no one realized it?"

I'm raising my voice too much and I can see Kayla is becoming uncomfortable.

"I'm sorry, Amy. I don't know who Mark is," she says. "Listen, I should really get going. I'm already late. It was nice seeing you."

It's obvious she's just trying to make an excuse to get away from me. I can understand why. I sound like Mark when he's angry.

"Kayla, wait!" I call out, but she's already brushed past me.

I know she's heard me because the street is quiet, but she's not stopping her gait. I don't call out to her again.

Great. I thought this day couldn't get any worse, but it did.

I race back home while my mind plays a million thoughts a minute.

CHAPTER 9

Has Mark really lied about the whole thing? So then, what was he even doing at Kayla's party? How did he even learn about it? Did he go there with the sole purpose of meeting a girl, and I happened to be the victim he found?

I feel sick. As soon as I arrive home, I turn on my phone. Three missed calls from Mark and a dozen messages. I don't read them. I can't right now.

Instead, I call Catherine. I need someone to talk to, and who can do it better than your best friend? Catherine knows when she's supposed to offer advice and when to just listen.

I tell her everything about Mark. The fact that she can't hide her shock only makes me feel worse, like going to the doctor for reassurance and getting bad news.

"Amy, I hate to be the one to tell you this, but you have to break up with him," Catherine says.

"I know," I say.

And it's the truth. I know there's only one ending to my relationship with Mark. Spoiler alert: It doesn't end up with us getting married.

"Well, are you gonna do it?" Catherine asks.

"Yeah. But first, I want to find out the truth," I say.

"Don't go down that path."

It sounds like a warning rather than well-intended advice.

"Why?" I ask.

"Sometimes, it's just better not to know. Plus, you're just gonna get tangled up with him more and more, and that can never end up okay. Just end things with him and go on with your life," Cat says.

"You're probably right," I say.

But even as those words leave my mouth, I know I'm not going to listen to her. I want to... no, *need* to know why Mark lied to me. I guess I'm trying to find a reason to rationalize his behavior. I know there's no excuse, but I want to believe he isn't the kind of person he's shown me he is on our last call.

Catherine is at work and I hear someone in the background calling to her. Being a reporter is such a hectic job.

"Amy, I'm sorry, but I'm gonna have to go," she says. "There's this case I'm working on and..."

"No no, I understand completely. We'll talk another time," I say.

"Okay. Good luck with Mark. I'll talk to you soon."

I thank her, and we hang up.

The ensuing silence in my apartment leaves my thoughts swirling like a tornado, booming in my head. It's time to call Mark and end this, and I dread it so much. I wish I could just do it over text, but I always remember that one article I read years ago that said you should never break up via text.

Not only is it impersonal, but it's also the cowardly way to do it. And yet, as I stare at Mark's name in my contacts list, I don't care whether ending things with a text is the right thing to do or not.

I think we've all been tempted to do so in the past, right? Not just breaking up, but declining an invitation, canceling plans, etc. It's so much easier when you don't need to hear the person's voice or see their face.

I'm sure of one thing, though—I don't want to see Mark in person. If I'm going to break up with him, it's going to be via phone. I dial his number and press the phone to my ear.

As expected, he picks up on the first ring.

Come to think of it, he *always* picks up fast. It's like he expects me to call. Like he drops whatever he's doing just to answer his phone. Even when it comes to texting. When I send him a message, it doesn't take longer than a minute for him to reply.

I'm seeing so many wrong things all of a sudden that I haven't seen before, and they bother the heck out of me. I may sound selfish, but I really can't wait to end things with Mark and start anew.

Being single sounds heavenly right about now. I can do whatever I want without having to explain it to anyone. I won't need to make plans to go out. If I want, I'll be able to sit at home in my PJs on the weekend without makeup and eat ice cream directly from the tub.

God, I've missed that so much.

All those thoughts can't have lasted longer than a second in my head before they're interrupted by Mark's voice.

"About time," he says.

I had expected him to be apologetic or worried, but all he does is makes me feel less guilty about wanting to break up with him.

"We need to talk," I say.

"Okay," Mark says in a defused tone after a moment of hesitation.

We need to talk.

Those four words are meant to instill fear in every man who is married or in a relationship. Nobody says "we need to talk" because they found the toilet seat up. It's always something big and bad.

"Why did you lie to me?" I ask.

"*I* lied to *you*?" Mark asks. I can almost imagine him pointing a finger at his chest and his eyes growing wide in surprise. "You're the one who's been dishonest with me, Amy."

Here we go again, the blame shifting. I'm not going to fall for it this time. I refuse to validate his suspicions any longer.

"Guess who I ran into on my way home from work?" I ask. Mark remains silent. "Kayla. Remember Kayla? The person who's party you crashed? Your childhood friend?"

Mark is mute. Of course he is. He knows what I'm about to say, and he knows he messed up.

"Do you wanna revise the story you told me about you and her?" I ask.

I can hardly contain the smile on my lips.

Mark still doesn't say a thing. I expected him to start weaseling his way out of this with a convenient lie, but that doesn't happen. I guess he's smart enough to know when he's caught red-handed.

"I'm going to ask you again, Mark. Why did you lie that Kayla is your childhood friend?"

"There must be some kind of misunderstanding," he says. "Kayla knows me."

I guess he's not as smart as I thought. He's already trying to concoct a lie. At this point, I'm losing patience.

"Mark, I may be naïve, but I'm not stupid. I swear to God if you gaslight me on this, I will block you, and you will never see me again," I threaten him.

He doesn't know that I plan on doing that anyway. I'm just trying to get the truth out of him.

He sighs on the phone.

"Well?" I ask. "How did you get there?"

"There was no grand plan or anything like that if that's what you're thinking," he says. "I saw people gathering at Kayla's building. I saw you. I was enthralled by your beauty. I had to talk to you. So, I went inside and joined. Nobody paid attention to me. There were already too many people in there."

"Jesus Christ," I mutter under my breath. "You followed me to the party?"

"I wouldn't say I followed you. I saw where you're going, and I was interested to see what was going on."

Now he's just twisting words. *I didn't lie to you, I just didn't tell you the truth.*

"You followed me to the party," I repeat. "You pretended to be Kayla's friend. You lied to me to get my attention. Do you realize how messed up that is?"

"What are you talking about? I liked you, and I wanted to talk to you, that's all. No need to make such a fuss about it."

He doesn't sound remorseful at all. If anything, his tone tells me that I'm the one who's crazy.

"No need to make such a fuss about it? Are you even hearing yourself right now?" I ask.

"What do you want me to do? Apologize for liking you when I saw you?" he asks.

"That's not what this is about at all. You *lied* to me to get what you want. That's sick!"

"When I lie, I do it for something good. What about you?"

"What?"

"You lied to me about flirting with the popcorn guy. You probably lied earlier today about work, too?"

"I did not! What the hell is wrong with you?!"

"Prove it!"

"What?"

"Prove to me that you didn't lie."

I only then realize that the blame has been shifted in my direction once again. Either I'm not good at handling arguments, or he's really good at getting the heat off of himself.

There's no point in talking with Mark anymore. He won't ever see what he did wrong. In his eyes, his actions are justified because he meant no harm and because they put the two of us together.

I'm suddenly exhausted, and I realize it's a fatigue that's been looming above me ever since I started dating Mark. I'm more than ready to cast those shackles off.

"This isn't going to work," I say coldly.

"What?" he asks.

"Goodbye, Mark. I wish you all the best."

I linger just a moment, enough for him to be hit by the realization that I just dumped him. By the time he starts shouting colorful insults into the phone, I press the red button to hang up. The last thing I caught was, "Don't you dare hang up, you lying bi—"

I stare at my phone, my hands trembling violently. Not even a few seconds later, it starts ringing. I swipe to decline

70

Mark's call and continue staring at it. He calls again. I decline again.

It gives me immense satisfaction to do that.

Over the next ten minutes, a flurry of messages and calls make my phone produce vibration after vibration.

Pick up your damn phone!

You're leaving me because of that loser popcorn guy, aren't you, you cheating slut?!

Two missed calls.

Answer me, you bitch!

Pick up your damn phone!

Four missed calls.

I can practically feel the anger coming out of my phone from those messages. I'm imagining Mark hissing and swearing as he types out these messages and calls. Then comes a message that makes my blood run cold.

Pick up, or I swear to god I'm going to make your life a living hell, you bitch.

I stare at the message, trying to convince myself that he didn't actually send that. At the same time, I'm seeing what a bullet I've dodged. This isn't even a bullet anymore. It's a frigging cannonball. Mark is crazy.

If he's this psychotic about a relationship that's still in its infancy, then what would he be like later on? I can imagine him forbidding me from having social media, talking to guys even if they're baristas or cashiers, and dictating how I dress.

Any lingering doubt I've had about whether this was the right call is cleared up. I've made the right choice.

I'm going to kill you, Mark's message comes, and it makes me feel even more uneasy than his previous text.

I don't need to take this anymore. He and I are done, and I refuse to subject myself to his abusive behavior any longer.

I block his number, and then I block him on all social media.

Then, I retrieve a spoon and a tub of chocolate mint ice cream from the freezer.

CHAPTER 10

It's been weeks, and I'm starting to forget Mark ever existed.

After blocking him, I seriously contemplated going to the police to show them the messages he'd sent me but, at that point, I was pretty much ready to move on and forget Mark ever existed.

I wish I could say I was sad after breaking up with Mark, but that wasn't the case. I did miss some things, sure, but those were things that had become a habit for me. It's always a shock when you need to cut something from your life cold turkey, right?

Anyway, I don't sit at home crying that Mark and I are no longer together. I might have done that before running into Kayla and finding out that he'd lied. For the most part, I feel relieved because I keep thinking about how close I had been to putting myself in danger with him.

Mark is clearly unstable, and he's not the nice guy he tries to represent himself to be. The monster beneath the cracks pokes its head sometimes, and he can't hide it. I pity the poor girl who falls for him in the future like I did.

I'm not looking for a new boyfriend right now. I think I need a break. A break and to rethink whether I want to keep dating the nice guys my mother always told me to find or go back to the bad boys.

With the bad boys, you know what to expect. You know you're getting into a troubled relationship that is potentially doomed from the start, and you're okay with that. But with guys like Mark? You go in expecting one thing and get something completely different, and that's why I'm so bothered by it.

Right now, I'm just enjoying being single. Either I've grown more mature so that I don't need to bounce from relationship to relationship, or the few weeks with Mark have really put a dent in my patience.

Either way, I spend the first week after the breakup, thinking about Mark. Not like missing him but worried I might find him waiting in front of my building or showing up at my work.

It's such a profound fear that I can't relax at all during the day, and at night, I have nightmares about waking up to see Mark standing above my bed, a menacing silhouette in the darkness. And every time he says the same sentence before I wake up.

"I'm going to kill you."

After a while, nothing happens. Mark doesn't make my life a living hell like he promised to. He doesn't show up to kill me or cause a scene, and I start to forget he ever existed. At this rate, he's going to become a story I tell to friends and family about a psychotic guy I used to date who threatened to kill me.

I'm sure I'll be laughing at the whole thing pretty soon. I just need to give it some time.

That's what I keep telling myself as the weeks go by. Until I wake up one morning, go about my day, and only toward the end of it actually remember Mark ever existed. I'm almost ready to get back into the dating waters again.

Until I come back home from work one day and find a picture of myself plastered to the door of my apartment.

CHAPTER 11

I don't even realize it's a photograph until I get close.

I figured it might have been one of the other tenants leaving a notice about refraining from making too much noise or something, but when I'm in front of the door, the key dangling from my hand, I freeze.

It's a photograph of me leaving work. With jittery hands, I reach for the picture, take it off the door, and stare at it. I already know who it is. I don't need to even guess. I haven't made any enemies like I did with Mark.

My other ex who beat me up is in prison, and he has no idea where I live, so even if he wanted to send someone to screw with me, he wouldn't know where to find me. Still, I try to find another suspect in my mind, anyone other than Mark because, please, please, for the love of God, I can't deal with him anymore.

Especially not now that he hates me.

I suddenly feel like I'm being watched. I raise my head from the picture and swivel left and right. I expect to see Mark standing there, grinning at me from the darkness of the hallway. No one is there. I'm just being paranoid.

Breathing a sigh of relief, I look back down at the picture. And then I do something that I'll regret for many days to come.

I flip the picture to look at what's on the back.

Honestly, looking back, I wish I had thrown the picture away and never looked at it again.

I know it wouldn't have spared me all the trauma I experienced later on, but a superstitious part of me, the one that's now wounded and broken, wants to believe it would have made a difference.

On the back of the picture is a handwritten message.

I'm going to make your life a living hell.

The picture nearly drops from my fingers. I look left and right again, now even more certain that Mark is watching me. How did he even get inside the building? Does he have a key?

No, that's impossible. Someone must have let him inside. He must have lied to someone on the intercom, and they opened the door for him. That doesn't make it any better. I'm going to have to leave a message at the entrance for the other tenants not to let anyone they don't know inside.

It takes me almost ten seconds to insert the key into the lock of my apartment door. I slip inside and lock the door behind me, hyperventilating. I only then get the weird feeling that I might have locked myself with Mark inside.

I spin around and observe the apartment. My eyes dart in various directions and I hold my breath, trying to hear any noise.

Nothing but silence.

For the next five minutes, I search every nook and cranny of the apartment to make sure Mark isn't hiding anywhere. The photograph is still in my hand. I whip out my phone and dial 911. I explain my situation as best I can, given the panic mounting in my chest, and they tell me they've dispatched a unit to my location.

For the next ten minutes, I pace around my living room like a caged animal, waiting for the officers to arrive. I've placed the photograph on the kitchen counter, and I stare at it, and when I can't stare at it any longer, I pace some more before coming back to it.

I study the handwriting on the back, squinting to find a hidden message. I then check out the details of the taken photo. How had I not seen Mark? How had he managed to hide and take my picture? Where else has he been following me?

He easily could have shown up at the office and caused a scene, and I would have been in a lot of trouble. I'm relieved he hasn't done it until I realize he's probably just trying to avoid getting incriminated.

But I have his picture here. If I'm lucky, the officers are going to find fingerprints on it and lock Mark up. I hope I haven't smudged the prints by touching the photograph too much, so I leave it on the kitchen counter as is.

Ten minutes later, someone rings my intercom. I double-check if it's the police, and when I confirm it is, I let them inside. I'm so agitated by that point that I want to yell at the police officers for taking that long to arrive.

I refrain from doing so because I need their help, and antagonizing them is not going to make them do things in my favor.

The two officers look confused when I start telling them my story, and I realize that I'm speeding too much because of the panic. I take a deep breath, regain my composure, and start anew. The officers are nodding while I explain everything, and when I'm done, I point to the picture on the kitchen counter.

"This is what you found on your door?" one of them asks.

"Yes. I don't know how Mark got in, but he put it there."

"What makes you think it was him?"

"Because it has the same message on the back as the text he sent me before I blocked him."

The officer nods, picks up the photo, and inspects the message.

"We're going to take this back to the police station," he says. "Is there anything else you think might be useful?"

"No, that's all. That's enough to arrest him, right?"

"It's still too early to say, ma'am."

"Too early?" I ask, trying to contain my anger. "Officer, listen. He followed me to the party where we met. He took that picture of me without my consent at my workplace."

"I understand, ma'am, but that's not a crime."

"You're kidding, right? He threatened to kill me. He's obviously dangerous."

The officer puts the photograph in a Ziploc and says, "We're going to dust this for fingerprints, and we're going to have a talk with your ex, 'kay?"

The tone of the officer sounds patronizing.

"That's all?" I ask.

"I'm afraid so. If we can prove he's the one who took this photo and that he's trying to harm you, we'll place him under arrest."

"But you have evidence right there." I point to the picture, losing my patience.

"We have a photograph, but right now, we don't know for sure if it's your ex or not. Let us do our job, and we'll sort things out before you know it."

I cross my arms. The police officer's words don't fill me with any confidence.

"Now then, is there anything else we can do for you, ma'am?" he asks.

"When are you going to talk to Mark?" I ask.

"We'll head there right away."

"Can you please just call me after you've spoken to him and after you have the fingerprint results?"

"Will do. And here's my number. You can call in case you remember anything else important."

He writes his number on a piece of paper and hands it to me. I thank him even though I feel like there's nothing to be thankful for, and then they leave.

I almost wish I took a picture of the photograph with my phone so I could scrutinize the details some more, but knowing myself, I would only drive myself crazy, so this is better.

I should have gone with the officers to Mark's place though because he will surely deny everything. Being there, I could have at least cornered him in a lie and given the officers enough reason to arrest him.

Then again, the whole thing might turn into a shouting contest. And, not to mention, Mark is excellent when it comes to shifting the blame. He might end up convincing the officers I'm somehow the one harassing him.

Besides, I don't want to see Mark ever again. Even going through this is too much. So, I continue living my life and hope the police will handle this.

Just another in a row of mistakes I've made that will cost me dearly.

CHAPTER 12

When I call Catherine to tell her what happened, she's in utter shock. She agrees with me that the police not being able to do anything is bullshit and that Mark can't get away with this.

I already know all that, but there's nothing I can do. I'm waiting for the police officers to call me to inform me what happened when they visited Mark, but they don't. I'll have to give them a call as soon as I'm done on the phone with Catherine.

Catherine asks me a bunch of questions I don't have answers to—how did he get inside; who let him in; can't the police do anything about it; when did he take that picture of me, etc? Honestly, speaking to her only stresses me out even more.

I'm glad when she tells me she needs to go because Rick is calling her, and I thank her for listening to me. She tells me to be careful and to keep her informed, and then we end the call.

As soon as that's done, I dial the number the officer had left me.

"Hello, is this Officer Daniels?"

"Yeah," he says in a curt tone.

"This is Amy. You came to my apartment earlier today about that photograph."

"I remember. What can I do for you, ma'am?"

His radio crackles in the background, and a tinny voice says something imperceptible.

"I want to know if you had a chance to talk to Mark," I say.

"We did."

"And?"

"He denies taking your picture and putting it on your apartment door."

"Of course he does. What about the threatening messages he sent me? He can't weasel his way out of that, right? Did you ask him about that?"

"We did. He admitted to sending you those messages in anger, but he says he did so because you wouldn't leave him alone."

"Wait, what?"

"Yeah, he says you wouldn't take no for an answer and, even after he left you, you continued to stalk him."

"That's insane," I say. "You don't believe him, right?"

"He had some pretty compelling evidence against you, ma'am."

My heart is hammering against my chest. "What kind of evidence?"

"Videos of you standing in front of his building, of you hitting him, and a few others."

"You can't be serious. Those must have been manipulated. I'm the one who left him, not the other way around."

"Ma'am, listen. He said he's not going to press charges against you as long as you leave him alone."

I can't believe this is happening.

"Wait, just wait," I say. "This is all wrong. He put that picture on my door. If you run it for fingerprints..."

The officer interrupts me. "We already did. We didn't find any prints there except yours."

"What?" That word has somehow become my most used word this year.

"For all we know, you put that picture up there yourself," the officer says.

"I did not! It was Mark! Why won't you believe me?"

"Ma'am, try to look at it from my side. Right now, he's got evidence piled against you. You have nothing against him except a picture with your fingerprints on it. You can see how that looks from my perspective, right?"

What is he saying? Is he going to arrest me? How did Mark manage to convince the officers that I'm the one stalking him and not the other way around?

"Listen, intentionally lying to the police is a crime, ma'am," the officer says.

"I'm not—"

"I'm going to let this slide because we have our hands full, but if we get another call from him that you're still following him around, I'm going to have to put you into custody. Do you understand?"

What can I say? I can't disagree with him, and trying to convince him that I'm not the bad guy here obviously won't work. Mark had planned this whole thing out even before we broke up. He must have been collecting evidence in case something like this ever happened.

The videos where I hit him must have been the ones where we were playful with each other. The one of me standing in front of his building was when I waited for him to come down.

It tells me just how sick in the head he is.

"Yes, sir," I skittishly say to the officer.

"Okay. You have a great day now."

As I hang up, I remain seated on my couch with droopy shoulders, the phone in my hands. I'm staring at the screen, and I almost expect Mark to send me a message.

He can't do it, of course, because I've blocked him. But if he were to send me something, there would be no words or anything like that. Just a smiley face to indicate how triumphant he is.

And to let me know this is only the beginning.

Chapter 13

Days pass. I do my best to forget the incident with the police as I go on with my life. I keep telling myself Mark is no longer relevant.

He's scared me sufficiently by putting that picture on my door, and the police couldn't do anything about it. I'm hoping that's enough to quench his thirst for revenge.

I got close at one point to unblocking him just to tell him he wins and that I'm officially terrified. I don't care that it makes me look pathetic. I just want him to leave me alone.

When three weeks go by and nothing happens, I'm certain Mark has moved on with his life. Maybe he's found a new girlfriend-slash-victim. I know this is bad, but I'm hoping that's the cause because then his attention will be diverted from me to the new girl.

Besides, it's not like I can stop that from happening. Someone is bound to fall for him like I did. He's charming when you don't know him. I can only hope the next girl doesn't go through the same stuff as me.

I've installed Tinder recently, and I've matched with a hot guy. His name is Tim, and he's a writer. We're supposed to have a date tonight, and I'm excited about it. I know there are a lot of weirdos on Tinder, but I'm not going to make the same mistake as with Mark—I'm not going to go in hopeful and desperate.

I'm going on that date with zero expectations.

It's an exceptionally good day. Not only am I going out with a hot guy, but I'm also told by Cindy that my performance this quarter has been more than satisfactory and that, if nothing changes, the promotion will be mine next month.

Things are finally falling into place where they belong.

After work, I go home and take a long, relaxing bath. I get ready for my date, which takes two hours, one being me choosing the appropriate clothes. Tim and I are going out to a quiet café, so I guess there's no need to go over the top. I opt for jeans and a nice shirt because I think I look pretty good in them.

Tim is waiting for me in front of the café—what a gentleman. We find a seat inside, and his humorous attitude dispels the fraction of nervousness that lingers in my gut. He and I hit it off immediately, and I just know this date is going in the right direction.

In my head, though, I'm reminding myself not to rush things. What's the appropriate way to end the first date if you want to take it slow? A gentle kiss? A hug?

I'm afraid that just hugging might give him the impression that I only like him as a friend. Then again, it's a good way to filter out the guys who only want sex. If Tim asks me out on another date, it will mean one of two things: Either he's very persistent, or he wants something more than just a one-night stand.

God, please don't let him be like Mark.

I suddenly realize, right there in the café, while Tim is talking about getting his Master's degree in creative writing, how much impact Mark has had on my life. It's been weeks since I've seen him or heard from him, and I still suffer from residual damage caused by him.

It's not fair to Tim. I'm not one hundred percent invested in this date, and it makes me feel guilty. I forcibly shove Mark out of my mind and dedicate all my attention to Tim.

"Hey, when it's tax season, maybe you can do those for me. I'll pay you, of course," Tim says.

"Tell you what. You write me into one of your stories, and I'll do your taxes." I wink.

He leans slightly. "I need to get to know you better if I'm going to do that."

He's staring at me like he's trying to gaze into my soul. He's a writer, so naturally he'd pay attention to things normal people don't. He's probably taking mental notes on how I smile, where my eyes are flitting, whether I'm crossing my arms or shifting in my seat, and so on.

It makes me feel naked in front of him but, strangely, not uncomfortable. I let him undress me in his mind because I know that the erotic part is only one of the many pieces.

"Well, I'd be happy to help you with the details outlining your new character," I say.

I like seeing his facial expression light up at the coquettish remark. Yes, I know I said I'd take things slow, but if there's one thing I learned from all my past relationships, it's that men don't need hints. They need in-your-face signals that are like flares in the night.

"I'd like that," Tim says.

Just then, a booming voice incongruously higher than the murmurs and the soft jazz music snaps everyone's attention to the entrance.

"Amy!" the man yells.

I don't even have time to consider who it might be when I pivot to the door and see a stranger staring at me.

Oh God, please, no.

I have no idea what this person wants or how he knows my name, but I can tell it's bad news.

"There you are, baby!" the man says loudly enough for everyone to hear as he strides in my direction.

He's wearing a beanie and a thick jacket. Everyone in the café is shooting him quizzical looks as he crosses over to the table where Tim and I are sitting. I look over to Tim and see a confused expression on his face.

The man falls to his knees in front of me and puts his hands together as if praying. "Please, just come back so we can talk. Please, babe. We can sort things out; I know we can."

"Uh, excuse me? Who are you?" Tim asks.

It's the same question I've been meaning to ask if I could force my vocal cords to cooperate.

The man looks briefly at Tim. "I'm her husband."

"What?!" I snap when I finally find my voice. "I don't even know who you are. Please, get away from me, or I'll call the police."

Everyone is staring at me, and I'm so embarrassed. I have no idea what's going on. This man is clearly deranged to come up to me like this. But that doesn't explain how he knows my name.

"Just come back home, please," he says. "The kids miss you. They haven't seen you in months. I don't know what to tell them anymore."

"You didn't tell me you had a family," Tim says.

"I don't! I swear, I don't know who this man is." I shake my head.

My eyes briefly fall on the rest of the guests in the café. They're giving me judgmental stares. A young girl has her phone out and is recording the whole thing.

"Please, for the sake of our children and the six years we've spent together, I'm begging you—come back home," the man continues to plead.

I can see distrust washing over Tim's face. I don't know what I should do first: Tell the man to leave me alone or concentrate on convincing Tim the stranger is lying.

"Amy... Baby..." The man's hand falls on my thigh.

"Get the hell away from me!" I shout as I shoot up onto my feet.

Tim is on his feet, too. For a moment, I think he's going to defend me, but I see him picking up his jacket from the chair.

"I think I should go," he says.

"Tim, no. Wait, please. I swear to God, I have no idea who this man is!"

But Tim's not listening. He's already taken his wallet out and is fishing out money. He proceeds to put it on the table, gives me a courteous smile, and says, "I hope you resolve everything."

"Tim!" I shout.

But Tim is already at the door. The stranger's hand gently touches my hand. He mutters something, but I don't hear it. It's as if something is controlling me when I swing my hand at his face.

My palm cracks across his cheek. I hear gasps and laughter coming from the crowd. The man is still on his knees, a hand pressed to his cheek. He doesn't look like he's in pain, only shocked.

I take my things and stride around him, bursting outside.

"Tim!" I shout, but he's already gone.

I'm left standing there, looking left and right at the passersby, my ears burning from adrenaline and embarrassment.

What the hell just happened?

The door behind me opens, and I see the stranger who pretended to be my husband slinking down the street with his head down.

Anger is piloting me. I break into a dash after the man. I don't care that he's taller and stronger than me. I want answers, and I'm going to get them one way or another.

"Stop, you son of a bitch!" I shout as I grab him by the hand.

He jerks it free and continues walking without looking at me. I run in front of him and block his path.

"I said stop!" I put my palms in front of him.

He continues walking, pushing me back, but I'm slowing his advance.

"Why'd you do it?! Who are you?! You ruined my date, you asshole! Answer me!"

I want to slap him again, but I refrain from doing so because I need him to be talkative.

"Leave me alone, lady," he says as he tries to sidestep around me, but I block his path again. His voice is deeper now, contrasting the one in the café that was clearly an act.

"No! You're not leaving until you tell me who you are and why you did that!" I insist.

He stops and looks like he's considering whether he should tell me the truth. He then shakes his head and says, "I'm sorry."

He tries to step around me again, but I block his path once more. This time, he looks at me with a hint of anger. I consider the possibility that he's going to be the one to slap

90

me this time, and it's nearly enough to make me back down.

"Why did you do it? Who are you?" I ask. "I'm not leaving you alone until you give me a straight answer. Do I know you?"

"No," he says.

That's a start.

"What, then? Why did you do it? I had a really great time with that guy, and now I'm never going to see him again, all because of you. You ruined my date, and I at least want to know why."

He sighs. I can tell he's sorry for what he's done.

He says, "Fine. I have no beef with you. Some guy paid me to do it."

"Some guy?" I ask.

"Yeah. He walked up to me, pointed me in your direction, and gave me fifty bucks to ruin your date."

You can't be serious.

"Where is he now? The man who paid you, where is he?" I'm almost hysterical when I ask those questions.

"He left, I guess." He shrugs.

"Where did he approach you? Which direction did he leave in?" I'm reciting the questions rapidly because I know I don't have time to lose.

"Over there." The man points across the street to an alley.

I don't waste another second. I run across the street, dash into the alley, and then across to the other side. When I'm out, I look left and right, ready to confront Mark, but it's already too late. He's nowhere in sight.

And I know now that I haven't seen the last of him. This is just the beginning.

A taste of things to come.

CHAPTER 14

I return home, tired and defeated. More than anything, an incessant feeling of panic clutches my shoulders.

I don't know anymore what I can expect from Mark. He's clearly not done with me. Not by a long shot. And when will he be? When he's ruined every date in my life?

Calling the police will yield no results. Mark didn't commit any crimes unless it's a crime to bribe a dude on the street to ruin your date. Even if I did call the police, he'd find a way to boomerang the blame back on me, and then I'd just be in more trouble.

He's been preparing for this. What chance do I stand against his elaborate plans to ruin my life?

Fine. If that's how he wants to play, that's how we're going to do it. Whatever he throws at me, I'll take it stoically. When he sees that I'm unfazed by his blows (even if I'm not), he's going to stop harassing me. It might take a while, but I'm sure it will work.

I barely manage to finish that thought when someone rings at my intercom. My back straightens in attention. I've just stopped being so jumpy recently, and now it's happening again.

Tentatively, I approach the intercom, pick up the receiver, and ask, "Who is it?"

"It's Catherine," a familiar voice says.

Relief washes over me. Thank heavens because I can really use a friend right now.

"Come on in," I say as I press the button to unlock the door and put the receiver down.

I'm too focused on the fact that it's not Mark at the intercom that I don't consider that Catherine has stopped by unannounced, and that doesn't sound like her. Fear suddenly floods me once again.

Without giving it a second thought, I rush to the door and lock it. I then stare through the peephole, waiting for Catherine to show up.

My apartment is situated in a way that I can see the entire hallway through the peephole, so when I see the light from the elevator appearing on the farthest section of the floor, I hold my breath.

Catherine walks out of the elevator and plods toward my door. I stare unblinking, waiting for another figure to walk out of the elevator, holding Catherine at gunpoint, perhaps.

That doesn't happen. Catherine's all alone. I guess I'm just being paranoid.

Before Catherine can ring the doorbell, I've already unlocked the door and opened it. Her hand stops raised mid-air. Our eyes meet, and I smile at her. I'm so happy she's here I want to hug her.

"Hey, Cather—"

"Did you really think I wouldn't find out?!" she interrupts me with a curt tone.

Her shoulders are tense and her hands balled into fists. What's going on?

"I'm sorry, what?" I ask.

"I didn't want to do this in person because I can't stand to look at you anymore, but I had to have closure on this. So, would you mind if I come in for a few minutes?"

I step aside and let her in. I don't know what's going on, but I'm not going to deny my best friend entry into my apartment just because she's distressed.

94

Catherine crosses her arms and barrels inside. She stops in the middle of the living room and spins on the ball of her shoe to face me. I close the door and take a few steps closer to her, but not too close. I feel as though she will tear my hair out if I invade her personal space.

"What's going on, Cat? I'm confused," I say.

She raises her eyebrows and lets out a scoff. "You're *confused?*"

I shake my head and remain silent.

Catherine's hands drop. Then she folds them again. "I can't believe you would do this to me. I trusted you. You were my best friend! I was always here for you, and this is how you backstab me!"

Her voice trails as she begins sobbing into her hands.

"Cat, calm down." I take a step closer.

"Don't tell me to calm down!" she screams and I back away immediately. "I can't believe you would do something like this!"

"Like what? Catherine, please just tell me what's going on."

A knot twists inside my stomach. I already know something bad has happened, and I can't shake the feeling that Mark has something to do with it.

"Stop playing dumb! I already know what you and Rick have been up to behind my back!" Catherine says.

"I swear I don't know what you're talking about, Cat. Please, just tell me," I say.

Catherine's lips stiffen into a thin line. She digs through her purse and retrieves her phone. She taps on the screen for a few seconds then hands it to me.

I'm too afraid to take it. I know I won't like what I'll see there, but I have to know. It's the only way I'll clear up this confusing situation with Catherine.

I reach for the phone and only then realize how badly my hands are shaking. It probably makes me look even more guilty, whatever it is that I supposedly did.

My fingers close around the phone, and I bring it closer to my face. I'm staring at a screenshot of a messaging history. It's between me and Catherine's boyfriend, Rick. My heart is beating so fast that I feel it up in my throat. I can tell right away that these messages are of an inappropriate nature.

Catherine tells me you have insane stamina, a message from me shows along with a winking smiley face.

Don't believe everything you hear. But I'd be happy to give you a demonstration, Rick says.

These were only some of the messages.

"Swipe to the next picture," Catherine says.

Those words make an anvil drop to the bottom of my stomach. There's more?

What choice do I have? I swipe to the next picture. There are more messages between me and Rick and some salacious pictures. Pictures of Rick's private parts sent to me and pictures of me revealing my breasts to Rick.

I recognize that picture of me. It's a picture I had sent to Mark when we sexted once.

"Oh my God." I look up at Catherine. "This isn't real."

"Swipe to the next one," Catherine commands.

"Catherine, listen to me, please. I never spoke to—"

"If you're going to do shit like this, then you're going to have to face the consequences of your actions,"

Catherine raises her voice. "Swipe to the next one."

96

She can't be reasoned with right now. I'll do as she says, and then I'll explain that these screenshots have been faked.

Swiping to the next page, I see more screenshots between me and Rick. These talk about how great the sex was and how I can't wait to see him again. We also talk about Catherine and make fun of her for not knowing we're doing this behind her back.

The scariest thing about these screenshots is that the messages look like they've really been sent by me because of the style, the punctuation, and the usage of smileys. It's so convincing that, for a split second, I question whether I really didn't text Rick like I claim.

Mark has put some serious effort into faking these.

I hand the phone back to Catherine and pray she will not force me to look at anything else. To my relief, she doesn't.

But then she says, "Oh, and there are audio recordings of the two of you having phone sex. Wanna hear it?"

"Please stop, Catherine," I plead with my hands over my ears.

I don't know how I know this, but I'm sure that the voice I'm about to hear really belongs to me, maybe of a time I had phone sex with Mark. Did he record me while we were doing so?

That sick bastard.

Luckily, Catherine doesn't play the audio. I wait a few seconds longer before putting my hands down.

I raise my palms defensively. "Okay, listen to me. I know how this looks, but you have to trust me when I say it's fake."

Catherine scoffs again. She looks like she's about to laugh in my face. "Seriously, Amy? You can't even take responsibility for your own mess?"

"That's not—"

"We've known each other since high school. High school! To think you'd do something like this to me after so many years of friendship."

"Cat, I swear I didn't do anything. I would never."

"Is this the first time you slept with one of my boyfriends?"

I'm so dumbstruck. I can't believe Catherine is accusing me like this. Is this even my best friend in front of me or someone disguised as her? Because this doesn't sound like Catherine one bit.

"How can you say that? Catherine, you're my best friend. I care about you," I say, tears welling up in my eyes.

It's an accumulation of everything bad that's happened today, and on top of that, Catherine's words are like knife stabs.

"Oh, don't you dare make this about yourself," Catherine says.

"Listen, I never sent those texts. I never even spoke to Rick. Mark must have faked them," I blurt.

"Mark? You're seriously pinning this on him?"

"Cat, come on. You know he wants to ruin my life. I already told you everything he did to get me into trouble. Just talk to Rick, okay?"

"I already did."

"And?"

"His story is even stupider than yours. He used the good ol' "I got hacked" excuse." She rolls her eyes.

"This doesn't seem suspicious to you even in the slightest? Look, I just got back from a disastrous date. There was a man there, and he—"

"Amy!" Catherine says my name in such a stern manner that I stop speaking immediately. She looks like a parent ready to scold her child. "Just drop it, okay? If the screenshots and the voice recording aren't enough, there's also a video I found on Rick's phone."

"A video?" I gulp.

"Yes, a video of you and him. I wish I didn't need to see it, but I did."

There's pain in Catherine's eyes. I've seen similar pain in her eyes once before, back when her boyfriend of three years left her for a coworker he fell in love with. It's the look of utter betrayal. The look of someone whose trust has been broken by the person they trusted the most.

And yet, looking at Catherine now, I can see the pain in her eyes is astronomically higher than the pain she suffered when her boyfriend left her.

It's terrifying to be stabbed in the back by the person you trust with your entire being and the person who knows you better than anyone in the entire world. Because, if they know you so well and still betray you, it makes you wonder if you're really worth anything.

"A v-video?" I ask, stuttering.

"Yes, a video. I have it on my phone. Wanna see it?" Catherine grins, but the pain is still visible in her eyes.

"No." I shake my head.

"I didn't think so. I hope the good sex was worth losing a friend, Amy." There's defeat in her voice, and it makes me want to cry.

Catherine brushes past me to the door.

"Cat, wait," I call out.

She stops and turns around, but I don't know what to say. You have to believe me? I swear I didn't sleep with Rick?

Catherine has evidence against me even if that evidence is fake. It's my word against videos, audios, and images. It's hard to dispute that.

Seeing that I have nothing to say, Catherine flashes me a weak smile, opens the door, and says, "Goodbye, Amy."

And then she's out.

Not even ten minutes later, I'm deleted and blocked by her everywhere. All our pictures together on social media are deleted. It's like we never knew each other.

I assume a fetal position on my bed and cry. I cry so hard that the muscles in my abdomen hurt. I cry harder than I cried when my dad died. I cry even when there are no more tears to shed because I've just lost my best friend.

And it's all Mark's fault.

CHAPTER 15

I've taken a day off work after that. I felt as though I wouldn't be able to get out of bed, let alone focus on eight hours of paperwork.

I hardly eat anything the following day. Even when my stomach rumbles with hunger, a persistent nausea prevents me from taking more than a bite. Even that feels like it's going to shoot back out of my stomach if I move too much.

The date with Tim is irrelevant in my mind. Catherine is the only person I can think about. The conversation with her replays in my mind over and over, driving me insane. I can't get her face out of my head. That face full of hurt.

I can't tell what's worse: seeing her in that state or knowing she blames me for it.

Throughout most of the day, I sleep. My phone is on, and so is the tone because I'm sort of hoping Catherine will come through and realize I did nothing to jeopardize her relationship.

I hate how I jump every time my phone dings with a notification, only for my hope to plummet when I see it's something useless from an app I don't care about or a newsletter I subscribed to.

When the following morning comes, I feel like a zombie. I get out of bed and hop into the shower. I spend a solid twenty minutes in there, enjoying the sensation of scalding water on my skin. By the time I step out, I feel so much better.

I feel like I'm ready to tackle today's work, but I hope the elation isn't only momentary. I still think about

Catherine, but the shock has abated slightly, giving way to the realization that this is now my reality.

When I reach the office, I do the usual—smile at my coworkers as I greet them, get my coffee and breakfast, and then sit at the desk to work. Not even ten minutes later, my manager Cindy approaches me.

"Hey, Amy. You feeling better today?" she asks with a smile.

"Yeah, thanks for asking." I flash her a courteous smile.

"Did you get sick or something?"

"Uh... yeah, I was feeling under the weather, but I'm all good now."

"Okay, glad to hear it. Listen, can I see you in my office when you have a minute?"

"Sure."

She thanks me and disappears. I wonder what she might want. Maybe a new client, or some updates from existing ones, or...

Oh, that's right. I totally forgot that a promotion is due. I know that nobody else in the company has attained the results that I have. The finish line is pretty much in front of me, and everyone else is in the dust, and that's why I'm so confident that this promotion is mine.

Well, that's one sliver of light in this darkness I'm experiencing right now. Hopefully, the extra pay is going to let me afford more things I've been eyeing lately, like those cute boots and heart-shaped purses.

I take a sip of coffee and head over to Cindy's office. She's on her computer, squinting at the screen, clicking something on her mouse. The screen's glow is reflected in her glasses.

"Hey. What's up, Cindy?" I ask.

She doesn't look away from the screen.

"Have a seat," she says.

I do so and wait as she does her thing on her computer. I wonder if I'll ever get to the level where I'll get my own office. That would be the dream.

Cindy rotates her chair to face me as the printer on her desk starts whirring, spitting papers out.

"So..." Cindy says.

She doesn't smile this time, and I wonder if she's having a bad start to her day.

"So," I repeat.

Cindy looks down at her desk then up at me, and I can tell she's uncomfortable. Damn, I already know what she's going to tell me. I didn't get the promotion.

"Is something wrong?" I ask.

Cindy ignores my question and says, "Your results were outstanding, Amy. I've never seen someone work as hard as you. Other employees look up to you."

"Thank you," I say.

Cindy speaks the next sentence slowly, as if searching for the right words, "That's why I don't... um... I don't understand.... How do I put this... You were on the right path to getting your promotion, and I'm just trying to see why you would do what you did."

My heart leaps into my throat.

"I'm sorry?" I ask.

Cindy sighs. She plucks the papers that the printer spat out and hands them to me.

"What is this?" I ask, mostly because my heart feels like it's going to burst out of my chest because of the suspense.

I look down at the paper and see pages and pages of familiar data.

"Is this for the client from Brazil?" I ask.

Cindy nods. "Yes. This is all the data we found on your computer that you planned to leak in exchange for monetary compensation."

My head snaps up. "What?"

Cindy is staring at me with a reticent look. I take it as a sign that I should read the stuff printed on the paper.

I scrutinize page after page. I can see a transcribed email in which I ask the client for a smaller payment than what they paid the company in exchange for me giving them all the necessary data. I've even attached some files, enough to pique the client's interest.

"What the hell is this?" I ask, looking up at Cindy for clarification.

"You should know, Amy. You're the one who sent it." Cindy shrugs.

"This is absurd. I never sent these emails. This has got to be a mistake."

"I'm afraid there's no mistake."

"You have to look into this. I swear I didn't send this. Maybe my email was hacked."

The good ol' I got hacked excuse.

"We've confirmed that the email was sent from your laptop, using the company wi-fi."

Cindy's cold tone is what worries me the most. She's always friendly, and right now, she's staring at me like I'm a junkie who's trespassing.

"Well, someone must have logged into my computer," I say. "Come on, Cindy. You know me. I wouldn't do anything like this."

"Look, there's nothing you can do to make this better, Amy," Cindy says. "This is hard evidence, and there's nothing that can refute that."

"Can you please just look into it some more before you make a decision?"

I'm sitting on the edge of my seat, and I don't even know when that happened. My entire body is shivering, and I feel like my lungs are going to implode.

"I'm sorry, Amy." Cindy shakes her head. Those words cause an iron ball to drop from my chest to my feet. "The higher-ups are already aware of the situation. We have no choice but to let you go. Now, given the nature of the problem, we're well within our rights to sue you, but I've convinced them to drop the charges out of respect for all the effort you put into making the company grow over the years."

"Cindy, please..."

"Don't make this any worse than it already is, Amy. You have until the end of the day to clear your desk. Now, if you'll excuse me, I have a lot of work to do."

She swivels her chair around to face her computer. I'm left staring at her a moment longer, the damned papers still on the desk in front of me. I'm trying to find a way to salvage this situation, but the conversation with Cindy is already over.

There's nothing I can say or do to fix this.

CHAPTER 16

I do my best to ignore my coworkers' curious stares and the whispers I hear from their desks as I pack my things.

They know why I've been fired. Nobody comes to me to ask me what's going on. I'm partly glad for that because I feel as though explaining what happened and then seeing their fake-pitiful expressions will only make me cry.

That's why I keep my head down the entire time. At one point during the day, one of the IT guys comes along and tells me to hand him over the laptop so he can scrub my accounts off it. It causes another jab on top of the already existing pain.

I don't realize how emotionally I've grown attached to that laptop until I can no longer use it. But my attachment to the piece of electronics is nothing compared to the cactus on my desk. I'm so distressed that I can't look at it, so I ultimately decide to leave it there.

It's probably for the best because it would only remind me of work. Right now, I don't need anything at home to remind me of work.

Walking out of the office is difficult because of the tears that blur my vision. I can see in the corner of my eye the receptionist Emily staring at me, but she doesn't wish me a nice day like she usually does.

On my way out, I absorb as many details from the office as I can. The moment I step outside, I will no longer be welcome here. It's safe to say I will never see this place again.

I can't believe how much I hated some of the things in the office. I miss them so badly right now.

The urge to call Catherine to cry to her is very strong, but I stop myself when I remember that Catherine and I are no longer friends. As soon as I'm out the front door of the office, I put my box on the ground, squat down, and bury my face in my hands, sobbing like a little kid.

I don't even care that the people walking by get to see me crying. None of them stop to ask what's wrong, and I'm grateful for that because I really don't have the strength to explain my predicament to them.

Some time later—it could have been minutes or hours for all I know—my eyes are unable to produce any more tears, so I stand. Just in time, too, because a security guard from my work (*former* work) steps outside to warn me that I can't stay here.

He's always been nice to me and now treats me like dirt. He's just doing his job, I guess.

I take my time dragging myself home. I have no reason to rush. I have the entire day in front of me, and I can do whatever I want, which should make me happy, but all I feel is a looming sense of defeat. How can I be happy when I have no job to support myself?

The financial noose is already tightening around my neck. I have some savings, enough to keep me afloat for a few months, but I'm still panicking. I hadn't planned on saving that money for rainy days. I mean, I had, but I also kind of thought I might one day get my own place and that the savings would come in handy.

The thought of splurging my hard-earned money makes me want to cry again.

As soon as I enter my apartment, I put the box I've been carrying this entire time on the counter and go inside the bedroom. I plop into bed and stare at the ceiling.

The silence doesn't help because it only accentuates my already raging thoughts. As I always do, I replay the conversation with Cindy in my head. I consider whether there's something I could have done differently.

Only then do I start to think about the actual problem—the emails with the leaked data.

I can only reach one conclusion. It doesn't strike worry or fear into me anymore. Instead, it makes me boil with unadulterated anger.

I'm going to make your life a living hell.

It was him. I know that much. It doesn't take a detective to figure that out. But I have no way to prove it. Mark is even more thorough than I thought he was. How did he manage to send an email from my laptop, from the company's location, without anyone ever suspecting anything?

I remember now.

That time he sent me an email. It must have had some virus or something, and when I replied to him, he was able to hack the laptop. That's gotta be what happened. There's no way he could have entered the company without someone growing suspicious of him. He must have remotely controlled my laptop to send those emails.

My doorbell rings, interrupting my thoughts.

I push myself into a ramrod sitting position, eyes wide. Was that the door or the intercom?

As if to confirm my question, I hear the doorbell again.

I jump on my feet, my breath held. I tip-toe to the door, and I'm suddenly aware that I haven't locked it. I stare at the door from the safety of my living room, waiting. My eyes flit around the apartment in search of a weapon. The only thing I can use is the vase on my coffee table.

Silence.

When I become too impatient to wait, I sneak to the door and gently lean forward to peek through the peephole. There's nobody there.

Feeling more confident, I open the door to observe the hallway with my own eyes. Just to be safe, I look left and right. Nobody is hiding to give me a jump scare. Then I look down, and I hear myself gasp. At first, I refuse to believe what I'm seeing, but then I come to terms with it.

The cactus that I left at work is at my feet.

I bend down to inspect it because this can't possibly be the same cactus from my office. No way. But when I pick up the pot, I see that it is. I recognize the shape. It's the same plant.

When the building is silent, I can hear the elevator whirring between floors when someone's using it.

And I hear that right now.

Mark.

I put the cactus on the floor and break into a dash to the stairs. If I'm fast enough, I can catch him before he leaves. I vaguely become aware that my phone is in my apartment, but I don't have time to go back for it. I have to catch up with Mark.

I race down the stairs. I don't even say hi to the old lady who lives next door. I make it to the ground floor just in time to hear the elevator closing. When I turn the corner, a figure slinks out the front door and out of sight.

"Hey! Stop right there!" I shout as I run after Mark.

110

I'm far too late, though. By the time I burst outside, Mark is nowhere in sight, and I'm left with the realization that he's once again one step ahead of me.

CHAPTER 17

I don't waste time wallowing in my own misery. I don't even think about the cactus anymore.

I mean I did, sure, for a few hours after I'd found it, and I contemplated calling the cops, but I knew it would only raise more questions and yield no answers. Besides, I have more important things to focus on right now.

I'm already browsing Indeed for new jobs. It's scary and stressful but also exciting. I now have a chance to finally look for something with better pay.

One thing that I liked about my (previous) job is the fact that the hours were flexible. The pay wasn't bad, either, but it was not as good as what I can get in other companies. In fact, most of my former coworkers who left the company did so because they got a better-paying offer—same position, mind you.

To be honest, some of these job ads I'm seeing offer higher pay than what I would have gotten with my promotion, and that's enough to boost my spirits. I also qualify for most of the spots I've applied to, so I'm hoping to get an offer back from one of them in the near future.

My prayers are answered just two days later when I get a call from a recruiter. He wants to schedule an interview, and I happily agree to come at his earliest convenience—which is the following day.

It's been a long time since I've done this whole job interview thing. I hardly even remember the questions they ask, so I go online and look up interview questions and answers to prepare. I rehearse in front of the mirror, especially focusing on smiling and showing my positive attitude.

No one can resist my amicable attitude in the work environment. That's why I never had any heated discussions that escalated. Unless the interviewer is a sociopath, I'm confident I'll do well at the interview.

The following day, I dress up and drive to the company. The interviewer is a polite and friendly man in his mid-thirties. His hair is slick and his suit without a single wrinkle on it. Everything goes well until he asks me what happened at my previous job position.

I've prepared for this question in the past few days, but I'm still unsure how to answer it. I decide to be honest and tell him that I got fired, which he can find out with a simple background check.

I don't tell him the truth about why I was fired, though. How do you think it will look to tell the interviewer I was fired because of leaked emails that I didn't send? Instead, I tell him I've had disagreements with higher-ups about the way they were operating.

The interviewer nods. I'm afraid he might see through me, but he proceeds to tell me about the company and the position I'm applying for. I ask questions in order to learn more about the position and to show my interest.

I leave the interview in a good mood and feeling hopeful. I buy some donuts on the way home because I've earned them. I'm already planning on applying to more jobs once I get home. There's no guarantee the one I interviewed for will call me back with an offer, and I also don't know if I'll hear from the ones I applied to.

I enter my building, take the elevator to my floor, and take out my keys. I stop dead in my tracks when I raise my head at the door of my apartment.

It's ajar.

You've got to be kidding me.

I can't do anything but stand entrenched in my spot, staring at the door, wondering if I might have left it like this when I left. It's possible. I had been nervous about the interview. It's perfectly possible that I didn't close the door right.

Except, I specifically remember locking it and checking to make sure it was locked.

Except, when I get closer to the door, I can see the lock busted and the tongue protruding out, confirming that I had, indeed, locked it.

Someone has broken inside my apartment.

I don't enter. That would be stupid of me. This time, I don't hesitate to call the cops. If it was Mark, I'll have evidence against him for sure. If it's someone else, well... better not to enter anyway.

The operator on the phone answers, and I give them my address and explain my situation. She says they'll dispatch a unit to my location, and I'm overcome by a sense of familiarity.

For the next ten minutes, I wait in front of the building. If anyone is still inside and wants to leave, they'll have to do it through here, and I'm not letting anyone slip past me.

It isn't long until the cops show up. I'm glad it's not the same ones from last time because I feel as though they'd roll their eyes and immediately discredit what I say.

"Good day, ma'am. You called us about a burglary?" one of the two police officers asks.

I wish the situation wasn't so stressful because then I'd be able to appreciate how handsome he is. Right now, my mind is on one thing only.

"Yes. Right this way." I lead them.

When we're in front, I point to the open door and let them do the rest. They walk inside, but strangely, their guns aren't drawn. I guess they think the burglar has already left.

I stand in the hallway with my arms crossed, listening for any commotion. I'm hoping to hear it because it means they caught the one who broke in. Instead, all I hear is the officers' voices as they talk with each other.

A few minutes later, I hear the handsome one call out, "Ma'am, you can come inside!"

I do as he says, and my jaw drops on the floor.

My apartment is in disarray. The furniture has been cut open and the sponge inside thrown all around the floor. The coffee table has been smashed into smithereens with the shards of glass in interspersing spots on the floor. All the decorative objects have been knocked off the shelves and broken. Dirt from plant pots is everywhere.

"Oh my God," I say as I raise a hand to my mouth.

The handsome police officer is standing in the middle of the living room. The other one is gone, but I hear shuffling from the bedroom. I don't even want to know what that room looks like.

"That sick son of a bitch," I say to myself.

"You have an idea of who might have done this?" Handsome Cop asks.

It takes me a moment to compose myself and answer that question.

"Yeah. My ex," I say. "Have you found any... uh, evidence, I guess?"

116

"We're still looking. In the meantime, if you can check if anything's missing so we can file a report, that'd be great."

"Yes, sir." I nod.

Just then, the other cop waltzes out of the room.

"Find anything?" Handsome Cop asks.

"Yes and no," the other cop says and then raises a small, transparent bag. "Found this under the bed."

I can see some brownish substance inside it, and I already know what it is.

"Ma'am, turn around please," he says.

"What?" I'm in utter shock.

"You're under arrest for possession of an illegal substance. Now, please turn around," the cop repeats.

"No, wait! That isn't mine! I swear!"

I realize that convincing the cops will have no effect on them only after I say those words. The cop is striding toward me, and I can see his shoulders tensing up as he prepares to tackle me if I offer resistance.

"Officers, listen to me." I turn to Handsome Cop. "My ex. He must have planted that there. I don't do drugs. I'm a law-abiding citizen and a hard-working corporate woman."

Except I'm no longer a hard-working corporate woman. I'm an unemployed person with a questionable history of relationships and no evidence to back up my innocence.

Handsome Cop's demeanor has suddenly changed, too. He repeats what the other cop had said, and I have no choice but to comply.

I never thought I'd hear the click of the handcuffs on my own wrists. I never thought I'd ride in the back of a police vehicle, either. My things are confiscated from me, and I'm put inside an empty cell. The heavy door closes and locks, and I'm left alone with my thoughts.

My life is falling apart right in front of me, and it's all Mark's fault.

I didn't think I'd be able to, but I start crying again.

CHAPTER 18

At least I don't need to share my cell with anyone. The last thing I need is to be locked up with some hard-ass, tattooed girl with a shaved head who's been arrested for armed robbery.

I toss and turn on the uncomfortable bed all night long, and only when I see the first slivers of light poking through the window do I drift into an interrupted sleep.

A bulky police officer rattles the bars with his baton and orders me to stand up. A lot of what happens next is a blur. I'm brought in front of the court where I'm asked some questions—am I a danger to other people; will I commit other crimes, etc? I'm then granted bail, much to my relief.

I can't spend another night in that prison cell...I just can't. I'll go crazy in there.

I'll be more than happy to drain my savings just to get out. I'll have to appear in court again in a few months, which is when I'll plead guilty to the possession of drugs found in my apartment. I'll then have to pay a fine since the amount the police officers found is classified as a misdemeanor.

Somehow, I believe Mark has thought of everything, every step of the way.

The next problem I'm facing is: How do I bail myself out? I obviously can't ask the guards to let me take a walk to my apartment so I can grab my credit card from my purse. I think about calling Catherine to do it for me using my money, but I then remember again that Catherine no longer cares about me.

Maybe Kayla? She's the closest person here who can do it, and I don't want to worry my mom.

I haven't called her to tell her what's going on, and I think it's better that way. I can already imagine how the conversation would go down.

Hey, Mom, I'm in prison.

Oh goodness! I told you those boys would be bad for you! But did you listen to me? No! Of course not!

Her reprimands would only make me more stressed, so I reckon the best thing to do is quietly bail myself out and not let her know about any of it.

If things continue going like this, though, I'll have to tell her the whole truth soon. I'm jobless. I've been arrested, and I'll soon have no money to pay for rent. That means I'll have to move back to Ohio to live with her.

Just the thought of it makes me want to puke. Not just the idea of moving back to Ohio—I really hate that state—but the realization that, instead of moving up in the world, I'm sinking.

It's very easy for me to slide into another episode of depression if I let my thoughts drift like that. Before I can do that, though, the cell opens, and the same bulky police officer from before says, "Get up. You're free to go."

I'm convinced for a moment that I haven't heard him right.

"What?" I ask.

"I said you're free. On your feet."

I'm too happy to hear those words to complain. I hop up to my feet, but then realization hits me like a speeding truck.

"Wait, there must be some mistake. I haven't paid my bail yet," I say.

120

"Somebody's already paid it for you," the cop says. "Look, I don't have all day. If you prefer to stay in here, I'll be happy to lock this cell again."

I quickly go through the open door because I'm too afraid he'll actually do that. Who could have paid for my bail? Nobody knows I've been arrested because I haven't told anybody.

Except...

"Your boyfriend must really love you, lady," the police officer says.

CHAPTER 19

I don't argue with the police officer or ask him any questions. I just nod my head and follow him to the room where I pick up the items they confiscated from me (It's just my phone, my keys, and my wallet).

On my way out, I keep my eyes peeled, expecting to run into Mark. He's not inside the police station. He's not outside, either. What's his move? He's obviously not done with me, even now.

I'm starting to understand. This was only a warning. Everything that happened before was, too. The next time I get arrested, it's going to be in a way that I'll be behind bars for years.

When I return home, I can see that the lock on my door is still busted. I go inside and I'm greeted by the same, horrifying mess as the one I'd seen days ago. It's been untouched since. I can see footprints in the scattered dirt from where the officers stepped.

I try to assess the damages to the apartment. When I finish paying for everything, my savings are pretty much going to be drained.

I'm so sick of all this. I can't take it anymore and I feel like I'm losing my mind. I'm not the kind of person who would ever think about suicide, but, in that moment, I picture myself in the bathtub with my wrists slit open and the water turning red.

I would never do it, though. I'm not at the stage where I would even entertain the thought of committing suicide. It was just an involuntary thought that forced itself into my mind.

Besides, if I off myself, it would mean that Mark wins. I'm not going to let him win. I don't care if I have to ruin my life to take him down, but he's not going to get the better of me.

I take out my phone, and the first thing I do is check the notifications. Nothing except social media. Seeing that, it dawns on me how alone and uncared for I am. No time for self-pity. I go into my blocked contacts and look for Mark. I promptly unblock him and start typing him a message.

You crazy fucking psycho. I hope you're fucking happy, you goddamn fucker.

I didn't mean for the message to sound so aggressive, but all the bottled-up anger and accumulated incidents are speaking instead of me.

After a moment of contemplation, I cool off and hold the backspace button to delete the message.

I hope you fucking die of cancer, you deranged piece of shit, I type.

This time, I simply typed that out because it felt so good to do so. I feel a little bit of satisfaction. Not nearly enough to satiate me, but enough for the moment. I delete that, too.

I hope you're happy. You turned my best friend against me, and you got me fired and arrested. Congratulations, you've ruined my life. You win, okay? Now please, just leave me the hell alone.

This time, I hit send. For a second, I contemplate whether I made a mistake, but the fury that envelops me tells me otherwise.

124

The satisfaction of sending that message bursts like a bubble and disperses. The pleasure is gone, and all I'm left with is a sense of defeat and emptiness.

Then, I hear a knock on my door.

Oh God, who could that be?

My mind reaches the worst possible conclusion, but then I calm myself down. It can't possibly be Mark. It might be the nice old lady that lives next door. Maybe she wants to tell me that she's noticed my door is busted, as if I wouldn't know it already.

There's no reason for me to squint through the peephole this time. The door can't even be closed properly, so I just swing it open and hope for the best.

And my heart sinks in my chest because Mark is standing in front of me.

"Long time no see, babe," he says with a Cheshire Cat grin.

CHAPTER 20

A scream catches in my throat. I want to slam the door shut in his face and lock it, but I can't because it's busted.

It feels like years since I've seen Mark's face—the face I've grown to hate so much—but at the same time, it's as if, only yesterday, we called each other pet names and held hands. Nothing in my life has ever felt so foreign and familiar at the same time.

"Stay the hell away from me!" I backpedal.

"Relax, Amy," he says.

It's the calm manner in which he says it that drives me up the wall.

"Calm down? Calm down?!" I ask. "How exactly do you suggest I do that? You ruined my life!"

"Stop being so dramatic, will you? Trust me, you haven't seen anything yet." His face grows dark, and I know he's not joking.

"What do you want?" I ask, my anger melting.

"May I come in?" he asks politely, but nothing about him seems polite.

"No, you may not," I say.

"Are you sure?" he asks.

"Yes."

But I'm not sure because the tone of his question says, *You are about to make the wrong choice. Are you sure you want to do that?*

"Well, that's too bad." He makes a forlorn look. "Okay. Well, I'll be seeing you around. Or not."

He turns around, and I quickly call out after him. "Wh-what do you want from me?"

I can't see his face because he's facing away from me, but I'm imagining him grinning because me calling to him in desperation is exactly what he wants.

He turns around and smiles. "I just want to talk, okay? Is that so bad?"

"We have nothing to talk about," I retort.

"Oh yes, we do. We have a lot to talk about."

"About what?"

"About us."

There's an uncomfortable moment of silence between us. Then, I'm no longer able to contain the laugh of ridicule that bubbles inside me.

"You must be out of your freaking mind," I say through laughter.

Mark looks unfazed. Why do I have a feeling he has an ace up his sleeve that's about to wipe the smile off my face?

"Can I please come in for a minute?" he asks.

He's not going to harm me physically. Not yet anyway. I'm sure of that because then I'd finally have something to use against him, even if it's my word against his. He would never put himself in that kind of danger.

Standing in front of him, I realize that I'm not staring at a person with insecurities and self-esteem issues.

I'm staring at the face of a psychopath.

Rather than answer his question, I turn around and walk deeper into my living room. Mark takes that as a positive answer and walks inside. My arms are crossed when I turn to face him, and I know I look defensive, but I don't care.

I just want this interaction to be over with as soon as possible.

"Yikes, what a mess. You might want to clean this place up a little," Mark says.

"What do you want?" I ask, ignoring his remark.

"Come on, baby. That's no way to talk to your loving boyfriend," Mark says.

"You're not my boyfriend," I say. "You and I are over."

"Well, I hope you're wrong. Otherwise, I just wasted one thousand dollars on a woman who's not my girlfriend to bail her out of jail."

I clench my jaw.

"Anyway, that's what I'm here to talk about," Mark says.

I remain silent as I wait for the grand reveal he's obviously been preparing for.

"You and I have been through a lot. I've done so much for you, and I feel like you don't appreciate it," he says.

"Yeah, I guess I should be jumping in happiness that you got me fired and made me lose my best friend," I say.

"You don't need a job, Amy. I'll take care of you. And you don't need friends, either. You have me, and I'm all you'll ever need."

He's getting closer to me.

"What do you say? I promise I'll make you happy, baby," he says as he caresses my cheek.

He's making my skin crawl.

I slap his hand away and step back. My heels hit the ruined couch behind me. I have nowhere else to retreat.

"You're sick in the head if you think I'm going to get back with you," I say.

Mark looks like he just got insulted in the worst possible way, but that expression quickly fades and he's back to his calm self.

"I'd rethink that decision, Amy," he says.

"Why?"

"Because if you don't get back with me, I'm afraid you might end up on the wrong path that will ruin your life."

"What are you talking about?"

"I'm just saying the police might find something else to incriminate you. You might end up in prison for a long, long time, and I doubt I'd be interested in bailing you out then. Or you might receive a phone call from the hospital informing you of your mother being in a fatal accident. Or you might get both." Mark shrugs.

"You wouldn't dare," I say.

"*I* wouldn't do anything, sweetheart." He smiles. "It would be all you. But that's why I'm here. I'm going to be your savior. You may not like it right now, but you will learn to be grateful to me for dedicating my life to you."

Tears are running down my face. I'm staring down at my feet, unable to bear Mark's gaze. I'm sniffling and shuddering.

Mark's hand gently touches my chin and pulls my head up so that I'm forced to look at him.

"I love you, Amy. I'll always love you. Do you love me, too?"

What do I say? If I tell him I love him, he'll know I'm lying. But if I tell him the truth, he might punish me for that anyway.

"Yes," I say because, just like the first time I told him the L word back, I feel as though I don't have enough time to think about my response.

130

"You don't," he says.

"I do," I insist.

"No, you don't. Don't lie to me. I hate it when you lie."

His hand stiffens on my chin, pressing it tightly. His face is contorted into a grimace. But then His grip relaxes, and the smile returns to his face. He draws closer to me so that our lips are inches apart. I try not to recoil even though I'm disgusted by him.

He whispers, "It's okay if you don't love me. You'll learn to. We have all the time in the world."

CHAPTER 21

My life is a nightmare.

A living hell.

If this is what I have to endure, then I'd rather be dead.

Mark and I are dating again. I've moved in with him and canceled the lease on my apartment.

His place is much tidier than mine. I'd even go as far as to call it sterile. It feels devoid of human touch. There's nothing to make the place look personal. No pictures, no figurines, decorations...

The only thing that makes the apartment look less like a doctor's office is the plant Mark keeps on his windowsill. I like plants, but not this one. I hate how it's the first thing I see whenever I open the door like a reminder of the life I have to live.

At least I don't need to worry about rent anymore.

What choice do I have? I can't let Mark ruin my life and kill the people I hold dear. That's what he would do without hesitation, I know it.

He doesn't love me even though he claims otherwise. He enjoys having me in his possession. He loves giving me attention and trying to make me feel special, but it's only because it makes him feel good.

If I don't react the way he hopes I would or if I don't show enough appreciation, he gets angry and punishes me by locking me in the closet. It's not just the way I react to things that makes him unhappy. Sometimes, I feel like he's just looking for ways to punish me.

For example, one time, he came home from work to see me wearing my hair in a ponytail. He had told me my forehead is too big for that, and then he locked me in the closet overnight without food and water.

Other times, the coffee I'd made for him wasn't sweet enough or was too sweet to his liking, so he would force me to stand still in one spot for four hours while balancing a tray full of glasses and plates.

God forbid I drop those things, which I did the first few times because my muscles could no longer take the burn. For every broken item, Mark forces me to inflict one cut on myself. It has to be deep enough to draw blood, but it also has to be on my inner thighs so that the rest of the world wouldn't see it.

I'm running out of spots to cut. The old cuts barely have time to heal before new ones have to be inflicted.

Another unsettling thing he does is he takes pictures of me from time to time. And not, like, snapping a photo while I'm doing something—instead, forcing me to stand by a wall so he can take a picture. He does that every couple of weeks as if he's taking progress photos.

I don't know what that's about, and I don't have the strength to care.

I've deleted all my social media accounts because I kept getting random messages from strangers. Since Mark checks my phone and only lets me use it when he says it's okay, whenever he found a new message from a guy in my inbox, he would punish me even if I never replied to them.

I'm miserable. I go to bed every night wishing I wouldn't wake up. I hate myself. I hate Mark. I hate him with such a passion that I want to take the broken shards of the plates I dropped and stab him in his eye sockets.

I get all sorts of violent fantasies about mutilating him, and they give me a reprieve from the reality I'm forced to endure. When he's not home, I allow myself to cry. It's the only thing I can do to channel the abundant emotions inside me and not go crazy.

Often, I think about Kayla's party and how I wish I'd never gone to it with Catherine. I wish I'd never seen Mark there because my life would have been so much different now.

I might have had a boyfriend who would not make my skin crawl, and I'd have that promotion at work, and I'd still be friends with Catherine.

I miss my boring little life.

Days turn into weeks, weeks into months. Is this going to be my life from here on out until the day I die?

Every day seems the same until, one day, on my 30th birthday, to be exact, someone rings the doorbell. Mark is at work, and I'm alone watching TV when it happens. I instantly sit upright. Nobody has ever visited Mark since I moved here, and even the buzzing of the doorbell sounds foreign to me.

I walk over to the door and open it without looking through the peephole. I think I'm so desperate to talk to someone else and to cry for help that I don't care who's on the other side.

That's why my jaw drops when I see Catherine at the door.

"Cat!" I exclaim.

It's been ages since I've seen her, and I just want to throw myself at her and tell her how much I've missed her and how sorry I am to ask her to please, please help me.

The stern look on her face stops me from doing that as does the big cardboard box in her hands.

"I heard you got back together and moved in with your boyfriend," she says coldly.

I open my mouth, resisting the urge to tell her I was forced to move in.

"Here. I wanted to get rid of these since I can't stand to look at them anymore." She nudges the box at me.

I look down and see some familiar things poking through the open flaps.

"These are all the things I bought for you over the years," I say. "Catherine..."

"Do whatever you want with them. I don't care." She shrugs as she leaves the box in my hands. "Since you already took my boyfriend, you might as well take all of this."

I want to cry because I feel like a worthless insect. "Cat..."

"I know I said goodbye last time, but this time it's for real," Catherine says.

She still looks hurt. Has she really come just to give me these things, or was she hoping we could work things out between us? No, the latter is definitely not why she's here. I can see it in her eyes. I'm dead to her.

"Catherine, we need to talk," I say.

"There's nothing to talk about," Catherine says.

"I didn't sleep with Rick. I'd never do that to you," I say.

Catherine had already turned to leave, but now she's spinning to face me.

"You're still going on about that?" she asks.

She doesn't silence me immediately, which means she's willing to at least listen.

I open my mouth, but then the elevator opens, and who steps out? You guessed it.

Mark.

He's carrying a wrapped gift, and when he sees Catherine standing in the hallway and me with the box, he smiles.

"Hello there," he says. "You're Catherine, right?"

"Don't mind me," Catherine says. "Amy and I are..." She looks in my direction. "...we used to know each other. Just came to drop off some things."

I'm convinced Mark will invite her in just to screw with me. In my head, I'm screaming at Catherine to get out of here because it's dangerous.

Catherine turns to leave but then faces me and says, "Oh, and happy birthday."

I feel like I've been punched in the gut. Not only am I celebrating the big three oh miserable, but my best friend has rubbed salt into the wound by coming by to say goodbye.

Catherine walks inside the elevator without giving me another look and leaves. Mark stares at the elevator for a protracted moment then walks up to me.

"Hi, babe." He plants a kiss on my lips. "Whatcha got there?"

Before I can protest, he takes the box from me and walks inside.

In it are clothes, jewelry, souvenirs from our trips abroad...

I am overcome with a sense of nostalgia and sadness as I look at each item. I remember the moment I got her those.

"Cute," Mark says as he pulls out a teddy bear dressed like a pilot with goggles. "I think this will look great on the shelf, don't you think?"

Even before I answer, he places the bear on top of the shelf so that it's visible wherever you are in the living room.

I can't disagree. Otherwise, he'll punish me. I know exactly what he's doing here. The toy isn't going to be sitting on the shelf as a decoration—it's a reminder of how I lost my best friend because I defied him.

It's also a warning that things will be even worse if it happens again.

Right now, I don't care about the toy. I'm just glad Catherine is not here anymore because I don't want to put her in any danger. Even if that means I have to continue living this kind of life.

"Since it's your birthday, I had an idea of what we could do tonight," Mark says, and I already know it's going to be something bad.

He gives me the wrapped box he was carrying earlier and orders me to open it. I do so reluctantly, devoid of any emotions. Any happiness I'm supposed to have about opening a birthday present is gone, destroyed by this monster.

My heart lurches when I see what's inside.

"You like it?" Mark asks.

I'm staring at the barbed wire sitting folded in the middle of the box. I'm afraid to ask what this is going to be used for because I already know I won't like it.

"I thought I'd make this birthday poetic," Mark says. "The barbed wire represents you being my property. It has thirty spikes because it's your thirtieth birthday. You're going to wear that tonight."

138

I'm not looking at him, but I imagine a shit-eating grin on his face. I'm staring at the tiny spikes. Not long enough to kill a person but long enough to break the skin and inflict pain. I find myself wondering how painful it's going to be.

I've grown somewhat desensitized to physical pain by now. The mental anguish is the real hell.

"Here, let me help you put it on," he says as he reaches into the box.

I stand and turn away from him. I strip out of my clothes until I'm completely nude. A single tear slides down my cheek as Mark approaches me from behind. I don't allow myself to whimper or beg.

The barbed wire goes over my head and slides down to my neck. I feel the spikes biting into my throat, burning my skin.

"Better clench your teeth," he whispers into my ear. "I'm going to wrap this tightly around your body."

CHAPTER 22

One night, Mark and I are having dinner together. I made spaghetti, which is his favorite. I'm waiting for him to find flaws and punish me. I have long since stopped trying to be his perfect girlfriend because, no matter what I do, I'll get punished anyway.

If he decides he is going to torture me, he will find a reason to do so. So instead, I'm just being myself and, when he inflicts his punishments on me, I take them stoically. I'm hoping he will get bored of doing so if I'm no longer showing pain, but my gut tells me otherwise.

He's a very creative sadist, and he always finds new ways to up the level of torture.

"Are you happy with our relationship, Amy?" he asks as he spins his fork to reel the pasta onto it.

It must be a trick question because he already knows the answer. Telling him the truth will earn me another punishment from him, but lying to him will only make things even worse.

I look up briefly to try to read his face, but it's impossible.

"No. I'm miserable," I tell him as I play with my food.

I have no appetite to eat. I've lost ten pounds since I started dating Mark again. I hardly recognize myself in the mirror. My face is sunken, my hair straggly, my skin pale.

Luckily, my body hasn't suffered so much. If I ignore the scars on my thighs, I actually look better than before. My ass is still plump, the breasts are only slightly smaller, and my belly is flatter. I wish I could appreciate it more, but I know that the way I've lost this weight is unhealthy.

And I know that if I ever get my life back together, I'll gain those pounds back and then some.

"I know you're miserable," Mark says as he puts some spaghetti into his mouth.

He chews slowly while staring at me as if thinking of ways to punish me tonight.

He swallows then says, "I think you're just unhappy because you feel like our relationship isn't going anywhere."

I'm staring down at my plate. I no longer try to talk back to him or prove my point. This is all a mind game to him, and he always wins.

"We should probably start thinking about the next big steps we're going to take," Mark says.

Is he talking about marriage? I sure as hell hope not.

I dare to look up at him. He has a smirk on his face.

"What do you mean?" I ask because I need to know what foul plan he's concocting this time.

Every time I look up at him, my eyes catch the plant on the windowsill. It's impossible to miss that thing.

"You said your mother always wanted you to marry a nice man and have children with him. I think she will be very happy when she meets me," Mark says.

Oh God.

He *is* talking about marriage.

No. No way in hell. I am never marrying this person.

"You don't look too happy, Amy," Mark says.

The smile is gone from his face, and his contours are twisting into barely perceptible anger.

"I just don't want to rush things," I say, gravitating my gaze back to the untouched spaghetti.

142

"You've had more than enough time to not rush things. But if you're not as dedicated and serious about us as I asked you to be, then..."

"No, I am. I just... I need some time to think, that's all. You blindsided me. Just give me a few days," I blurt.

Mark laughs. "We're not going to have the wedding right away, silly. You have to become my fiancé before you become my wife."

Me? His fiancé and wife? I want to puke at that thought.

"Okay," I simply say, hoping he won't detect my disgust.

"Good."

Something stirs inside me, caused by this entire conversation. Up until tonight, I've given up, and I've come to terms with the fact that this is my life. Mark's talk of marriage has made me realize one thing.

Things are only going to get worse and worse until I can no longer take them.

I think I've reached my limit. He's pushed me to it, and I'm at a point where I don't care anymore what will happen to me. That's why something activates inside me that urges me to stand up to this asshole, even if it means getting into more trouble.

Everything that's transpired in the last few months replays in my head.

My date with Tim that he'd ruined.

Turning Catherine against me.

Getting me fired.

Framing me to get arrested.

Forcing me to date him. To *date* him!

I have freaking had it. I don't care what he does to me anymore. In the end, is life in prison really going to be as bad compared to what I'm going through right now?

Absolutely not. I'd rather spend the next fifty years incarcerated but knowing this man is dead than to continue giving him the pleasure of torturing me.

That settles it. I'm going to end this.

But I can't do it right now. He's bigger and stronger, and there's no way I can harm him like this. I could slit his throat while he sleeps.

No, that would be too easy.

I want him to suffer. I want him to cry like I've cried. I want him to beg me to let him go like I've begged and for me to ignore his pleas.

Mark drops the fork into the mound of spaghetti onto his plate, pushes his chair back to stand, and says, "The food is too salty."

I drop my own fork and stand up. I'm not surprised he's found something wrong with the food.

I don't cry or beg as he punishes me tonight, and he's really trying extra hard to make me cry. I'm holding on to my anger because that's what I'm going to use against him.

Just you wait, Mark.

CHAPTER 23

But what would I do to turn the tables around? Mark is too smart, and he's ahead of me by at least two steps.

If I want to outsmart him, I need to do something he would never expect from me.

Well, he wouldn't expect me to slit his throat in his sleep.

What he would expect, though, is for me to look for a way to get rid of him. I'm sure he's already taking all the precautions he can to keep tabs on me. The longer I wait, the more control I'll lose until I end up shackled to the kitchen with barely a few feet of free movement.

It sounds dramatic, but I'm pretty sure it's something that can very much happen in the future. Mark is already slowly taking away my freedom.

First, he forced me to install a tracking app on my phone. Then, he started restricting my phone time and who I can talk to. Then, I lost the privilege of being outside the apartment for longer than three hours (because I was once late home for one minute).

Just two days ago, he aloofly mentioned how he doesn't see a reason for me to use a phone when he has one. He hasn't taken it away yet, but once he does, I'm pretty much going to be blind and deaf. He'll have me in the palm of his hand, and I'll have no way to obtain information or contact the outside world.

He's trying to do all of this gradually so that I don't see the change and start rebelling, but he's doing it too fast. I see everything he does.

And besides, like I said earlier, I don't care what happens to me. If I have to kill him and go to prison, I will.

But I want to try to avoid that route, if possible. I want to get rid of him and salvage whatever remains of my broken life. I won't be able to do that by killing him.

I've thought about it a million times. If that were to happen, I'd be arrested, and the judge would see the defendant being a woman who got fired from her job for leaking emails, got arrested for drug possession, and then killed her boyfriend who paid to bail her out and let her move in.

Mark would be painted as the victim, and I would be called the monster. It wouldn't matter what he did to me.

People like him are smart, but they also tend to slip from time to time. I just need to give him a little push to make that happen. I decide to wait until he goes to work.

That's when I start snooping around the apartment under the guise of cleaning. I'm not very thorough when I clean, but I decide to be like that now.

I look in obvious spots first. When I find nothing, I look for more inconspicuous hiding spots. What exactly am I looking for anyway? I don't even know myself. Just something I can use against Mark, whether it be evidence or something to blackmail him.

Two hours later, the apartment is pretty much spotless— the shelves cleaned of all the dust, the floor shiny. And yet, I still have no evidence. My back and knees hurt, but I'm nowhere close to giving up.

There's gotta be something here. People like Mark love to keep souvenirs or something, and I'm sure he already has experience with these things.

146

I've flipped through every page of every book, checked under every object, felt every inch of the floor for a loose board.

Nothing.

I go through the entire apartment one more time. Come on, give me something, damn it. A hollowed-out book with evidence inside or a hidden safe, anything really.

But there's nothing. I'm exhausted. The apartment is spotless, and that should at least give me a feeling of satisfaction, but it doesn't. When Mark comes home, he's going to notice that I cleaned, and that's only going to inspire him to look for a spot I missed so he can punish me.

That's the least of my worries right now.

I lean on the windowsill and stare out at the street. Maybe he doesn't keep the evidence inside the apartment. Maybe it's inside his car.

My mind races as I try to find a way to search his car without arousing suspicion. My gaze falls on the stupid plant that I've been forced to watch every day ever since I moved here. My eyes drift away from the plant, but then they bounce back to it. And that's when it hits me.

It's a *fake* plant.

How have I never noticed that before? A fake plant. And it's the only plant in the apartment. Mark never waters this thing, and he's never asked me to do it, either.

Am I so desperate to find something that I'm seeing things that aren't really there?

I reach toward the plant and jab a finger inside the dirt. The tip of my finger comes in contact with something hard, so I gently sweep the dirt aside and notice a lighter-colored hard material around the root.

Cardboard.

I guess Mark must have tossed some dirt on top of the fake material to make it look more real.

Or maybe it's to conceal something else.

I close my fingers around the plant and gently pull it up. Dirt cascades off the cardboard onto the windowsill and the floor. I don't care. I have more than enough time to clean it up later. As I lift the plant, I can see that a much smaller pot is actually holding the plant, not the one I've been seeing.

I place the small pot on the windowsill and then peer down into the big pot. A plastic bag lies at the bottom with grains of dirt covering it. But even before I take a proper look, I can see that I've scored big.

Something is just under the plastic bag. Something Mark's been hiding this entire time.

As carefully as I can, I grab the edges of the plastic bag and lift it out so as to not scatter the dirt. I put it on the windowsill and avert my attention back to the pot.

Bingo.

At the bottom of the pot is a bevy of photographs and news article clippings.

CHAPTER 24

I feel like a kid on Christmas morning.

Grabbing the pot with both hands, I sit on the floor and overturn it to spill out all the things inside. I then set the pot aside since it's no longer useful for the moment.

I want to gaze at all the items at once because excitement is getting the better of me, but I control myself. I start to look through Mark's... memorabilia.

The first thing I take to look at is a photograph of a beautiful woman. She's smiling at the camera. Had I run into this picture on Instagram while mindlessly scrolling social media, I would have stopped to admire her perfect teeth, the lush, brown hair, and the pair of blue eyes that further accentuate her beauty.

Now, all I do is wonder who she is.

The next few photographs are of her, too, but in each of them, she looks more and more gaunt. Gray strands decorate her straw-like hair. There's a small scar on her cheek and a bruise on her neck. The smile gradually fades until she's staring at the camera with pleading eyes.

My heart is racing inside my chest as I stare at that last picture. The background is white, and I recognize it immediately.

It's the wall Mark makes me stand against whenever he takes pictures of me.

He's snapping photos of me because I'm his next victim. He's going to add my pictures to his collection as soon as I'm dead.

A cold wave washes over me, and I suppress it to focus on the task at hand.

The next thing I find is a cut-out of a newspaper article.

WOMAN FOUND DEAD INSIDE HER APARTMENT

Earlier today, police discovered the body of 26-year-old Adrienne Mendoza inside her apartment. According to the police, the other tenants had complained for days about a smell coming from Mendoza's apartment, but she refused to open the door. Mendoza's mother had also confirmed that Adrienne had not answered her phone in days.

Police were sent for a welfare check when they discovered Mendoza in her bathtub. The cause of death was suicide.

"I just don't understand why she would do it," Mendoza's heartbroken mother said. "She's always been such a happy, positive girl. I had noticed she'd changed in the past few months, but I'd thought she was just tired from working too hard."

Mendoza's boyfriend, who chose to remain anonymous, said the following, "I don't know how I'll ever recover from this. I had told her to seek help or take time off work so she can focus on her mental health, but she refused to listen. It's my fault. I should have done more."

The rest of the article talks about suicide prevention, but my mind is entangled in the paragraph mentioning Adrienne Mendoza's boyfriend. It had to have been Mark. Why else would he keep pictures of her? Moreover, how would he even have obtained close-up shots of her?

This is very suspicious.

150

I move on to the next piece of evidence. It's more pictures of another girl. This one is not as model-beautiful as Adrienne, but she's so cute you can't stop staring. Something uncomfortably clenches my heart because I know somehow, deep inside, that the girl in the picture is no longer alive, just like Adrienne.

Sure enough, every subsequent picture of the girl shows her in a more deteriorated state. Unlike Adrienne, this girl had gained a lot of weight. Her face is dotted with rashes, and tufts of her hair are gone, revealing bald patches. I find myself wondering if it was from the stress or because of a punishment Mark had inflicted on her.

The cut-out of the article I find next is very similar to the one describing Adrienne Mendoza's death. The name of this girl was Mary Campbell, and she was only twenty-two years old when she died by swallowing a bunch of pills.

Adrienne Mendoza. Mary Campbell.

I have to memorize their names so I can investigate what really happened to them.

Did they really kill themselves, or did Mark do it? Either way, he's responsible for it because, even if they committed suicide, he drove them to do it.

The next victim's name was Faith Barnaby. The article describing her death is different than the first two.

WOMAN KILLED IN SELF-DEFENSE AFTER ATTACKING BOYFRIEND WITH KNIFE

A 24-year-old Faith Barnaby was fatally stabbed yesterday by her boyfriend, who chose to remain anonymous for this article. After having a mental breakdown, Barnaby lunged at her boyfriend with

151

a kitchen knife and stabbed him three times. Fearing for his life, Barnaby's boyfriend delivered a fatal stab wound to her throat.

"She'd been unstable for a while," the boyfriend said. "I had told her to get help because she obviously needed it, but she always said she was fine. I know she meant me no harm. She just wasn't herself anymore. I'm really sad that it had to come to this."

Another anonymous boyfriend, huh? What a load of bull.

I think I can pretty much recreate in my head what happened between Mark and Faith. She had had enough, so she decided, screw it, I'm going to kill him. She tried to do it, and she even got close—unless he delivered those three stab wounds to himself to look less suspicious—but then he overpowered her.

That tells me what I've been afraid of this entire time: This isn't Mark's first time doing this, and he's ready for me to rebel against him.

I had thought he might not expect such a thing from me, but Faith's story confirms otherwise. Not all of the girls were driven to suicide. Some of them wanted to go out with a bang—and they did.

What happened with Faith most likely was that she waited too long to act. Her attempt to break free was an act of desperation, not a calculated move. That's why I think I still have the upper hand.

Especially now that I know what Mark is capable of.

I'll admit I'm more afraid of him now, but that won't impact my decision to get rid of him.

Adrienne Mendoza. Mary Campbell. Faith Barnaby.

I recite those names in my head over and over. When I'm sure I won't forget, I scoop up all the photographs and articles and put them back in the pot. I place everything back exactly how it was and get rid of the dirt that I allowed to fall from the cardboard.

I spend the next hour or so going through the apartment to make sure I haven't left anything out in the open that might tell Mark what I've been up to.

Adrienne Mendoza. Mary Campbell. Faith Barnaby.

The door opens. Mark walks inside. "Hi, babe."

"Uh, hi. You're home early," I say and immediately realize what a mistake it is to say that.

Those are the words of every woman who has ever been caught by their husband doing something bad like cheating.

Mark's head pivots left and right, and he suspiciously looks around the apartment.

"Hm," he says.

"What's wrong?" I ask.

My heart is hammering in my chest.

"Something's different. Did you do something with the apartment?" he asks.

"I've been cleaning," I say.

It comes out too smoothly from my mouth as if I've been practicing how to say it. It's not a lie, though.

Mark's head mechanically moves from one direction to the other, slowly scanning the living room. I'm trying not to look suspicious as I stand, waiting for his verdict.

His eyes fall on the fake plant.

And they linger on it.

He squints, and I know, in that moment, he's figured me out.

"The place looks spotless. See? You're already becoming a good future wife," he says with a grin and waltzes into the bathroom.

I take the moment to breathe a sigh of relief, my legs feeling like they've been cut off.

Adrienne Mendoza. Mary Campbell. Faith Barnaby.

I can't forget those names.

This is no longer just about my safety anymore. It's about giving those girls some justice.

Mark is going to pay for what he's done.

CHAPTER 25

The following day, Mark sends me to buy groceries while he's at work. He doesn't let me look for work. He wants me to stay at home and be a housewife forever.

Or however long it will take until he drives me to kill myself.

Before buying groceries, I go to a nearby café. I ask to use the bathroom, and I tape my cell phone under the sink. If Mark checks where I am, he's going to see that I'm at the café.

I slip outside and thank the waiters for letting me use the bathroom. I then go to the closest electronics shop and buy the cheapest voice recorder. I pay in cash because I don't want Mark to track what I've been buying.

Almost an entire hour has passed since then, so I hurry back to the café and ask to use the bathroom again. The waiter gives me a dirty look and, for a moment, I think he might refuse me. He then nods, and I thank him.

I enter the bathroom and feel around the underside of the sink and...

It's gone! My phone is gone!

My heart lurches, and I bend down.

It's still here, I've just been touching the wrong spot. I sigh in relief, my hands trembling violently. On my way out, I thank the waiter again and then finally go to buy groceries.

I've hidden the voice recorder in my bra. Mark is predictable for the most part and has never asked to see what's in my pockets, but he does tend to throw in a surprise inspection from time to time, just to keep me on my toes.

I think it's his way to check whether I'm hiding something from him.

I'm not going to let him fool me. Not when I have a concrete plan.

When I return home, the first thing I do is play around with the voice recorder to memorize how to start recording. I also record myself speaking from various distances to make sure it can catch everything clearly.

Luckily, it's pretty good quality.

I hide the voice recorder under the teddy bear from Catherine. It still pains me to look at it, but I'm glad it's here and I can use it to my advantage.

I then make dinner while waiting for Mark to come home. I went over the plan in my head a dozen times over. I'll confront him about the three girls and try to get a confession out of him.

I'll be open about finding the evidence, which will earn me some severe punishment—probably worse than anything I've gotten so far—but I don't care. As soon as I have his confession on the voice recorder, I'm going to grab the evidence if I can and alert the police.

He might move the pictures and articles elsewhere, but it won't matter. I just need to tell the cops to look into the cases of Adrienne, Mary, and Faith, and they're going to find a connection with Mark.

"Do I smell spaghetti?" Mark asks when he comes home.

I'm not going to be polite or friendly with him. That would only arouse suspicion. The only reason why I've made spaghetti for him is because I want him in a good mood when I start questioning him.

He kisses me on the cheek, and I act as cold as usual. I cringe whenever he touches me, so I don't really need to put much effort into faking it.

Every day I wonder how he can live like this. He obviously knows I'm disgusted by him, but he still forces me to live with him. He doesn't care about my feelings, I get that, but shouldn't he at least care about his own?

I think he simply enjoys inflicting pain on the women he dates.

"It'll be ready in about ten minutes," I say atonally.

"I'm gonna take a shower," he says.

The moment he's in the bathroom, I slip inside the living room and retrieve the voice recorder from underneath the teddy bear. I press the record button and make sure it's on before hiding it back under the bear.

The guy who sold it to me said it can record up to one hour, and I think that's more than enough time to get everything I need.

I do it just in time, too, because Mark comes out of the bathroom. He strides into the bedroom and comes out again three minutes later, dressed in sweatpants and a t-shirt.

I set the food on the table and wait for him to join me.

"Smells good," he says.

He rarely compliments anything I do. It's mostly criticism that I hear from him, like how my skin is looking bad and my hair is messy and my belly rolls are visible and my breasts are saggy, and my back is hunched, etc.

I've learned to deflect those kinds of comments. I'm not going to let a nobody like Mark dictate how I feel about myself. That's something he'll never take away from me, no matter how broken I am.

We start eating. For a few minutes, only the sound of our forks clinking against the plate and the squelching of the spaghetti fill the room. I don't have too much time, so I have to ask my questions fast. I prepare myself to confront him about the dead girls.

Adrienne Mendoza. Mary Campbell. Faith Barnaby.

I put my fork down and straighten my back. He notices this and stops eating.

"Something wrong?" he asks.

I take a deep breath. "We need to talk."

CHAPTER 26

"Oh?" he asks as he shovels a forkful of spaghetti into his mouth.

The way he asks that question makes it sound like *how dare you think you have the right to ask me anything without permission.*

He chews for a few seconds, swallows, then says, "What do we need to talk about?"

I lean my elbows on the table. "About Adrienne, Mary, and Faith."

That sentence was supposed to evoke a reaction out of him—eyes growing wide, jaw to stop chewing, shoulders tensing up, or anything really.

Mark instead continues chewing, then jabs some more pasta on his fork and brings it to his mouth. The lack of reaction is disconcerting.

"What do you want to know about them?" he asks.

I had expected him to become aggressive, so I'm so stunned at his blasé reaction that I don't know what to say next.

Pull yourself together. Now's your chance to get that confession.

"Who were they?" I ask.

"My ex-girlfriends." Mark is continuing to eat spaghetti.

Cold sweat envelops the nape of my neck and palms.

"What did you do to them?" I ask.

He continues chewing then smiles and shrugs.

Say you killed them so I can go to the police, you sick bastard.

"Did you kill them?" I ask.

"I killed one in self-defense for losing her mind and trying to kill me. The other two offed themselves."

I don't know if this is good enough for evidence. It might be, but I have to keep pushing just to be on the safe side.

"That's not true, is it, Mark?" I ask. "Adrienne Mendoza and Mary Campbell didn't kill themselves. You drove them to do it. And Faith Barnaby attacked you because you were blackmailing her like me. Isn't that right?"

Mark swallows the bite in his mouth, puts the fork down, and dabs his sauce-stained lips with a napkin.

"Yes," he says. "You're right. I blackmailed them all just like I'm blackmailing you. I tried to be the perfect boyfriend and treated you all like queens, but all you ungrateful sluts repaid me by ending the relationship. I couldn't have that. I tried to make them see they were wrong, but they refused. I gave them a choice. They chose to end their lives."

That's right. Just keep talking.

"You're lying to me, aren't you?" I ask. "You never cared about making them see they were wrong. Your goal all along was to torture them until you got bored, and once that happened, you'd wait for them to commit suicide. Isn't that right?"

Mark smiles. "You're not as stupid as I thought you were, Amy. You might actually be the one who's going to see things my way. I think you and I are going to be very happy married."

"Am I going to end up like them? Like Adrienne, Mary, and Faith?"

"You mean dead? That's completely up to you, babe. If you misbehave, I am going to have to punish you."

160

"You're going to keep punishing me anyway. You and I both know that."

"That's unfair, Amy. I never punish my girlfriends without a reason. For example, I'm going to have to punish you for snooping around my things."

I remain silent. Me confronting him about the dead girls was going to reveal that I knew the truth either way. I had already prepared myself for it. I just need to survive until tomorrow, and as soon as he goes to work, I'm heading to the police.

I have more than enough evidence to incriminate him. My eyes fall on the teddy under which I've left the voice recorder. When I look back at Mark, he's staring at me intently and smiling.

He reaches one hand into his pocket and pulls something out. My eyes grow wide and terror envelops me.

"Looking for this?" he asks as he dangles the voice recorder in his hand.

The expression on my face seems to only widen his smile.

Mark says, "You see, I already knew you touched my things, Amy. I knew it the moment I saw the plant slightly out of place. That big, pointy leaf? It always faces the window. You forgot to move it back. And when I looked through my mementos, I noticed they'd been moved. Naughty girl. Oh, and I forgot to mention that I might have placed a camera inside the apartment."

Shit. I'm screwed. I'm so screwed.

He puts the voice recorder back into his pocket and leans forward. "The punishment tonight is going to be so very bad. It'll be extremely painful. I hope you're ready for it because you won't ever be the same after tonight, and you'll definitely never get any crazy ideas like this."

I have no choice. I have to kill him. It's the only way I'll ever be free of this psycho.

But I've lost the element of surprise. What do I do? Jab a fork in his eye? He can overpower me with one hand tied behind his back.

He stands up. It's starting.

I grab my fork and push my chair back. Mark is making his way around the table, his arms and shoulders tense as he prepares to punish me.

"Stay back!" I point the fork in front of myself.

He stops for a moment and lets out a peal of laughter.

"Really, Amy?" He spreads his arms. "Put that thing down. You're going to hurt yourself."

"Don't come any closer, or I swear I'll stab you," I say.

I'm holding the fork so tightly that my hand hurts.

Mark is staring at me with an amused expression on his face. I can see his knees bending as he prepares to lunge at me, but I'm too slow to react. His hand has already closed around my wrist and is twisting it. I yelp in pain as I drop the fork.

He backhands me across the mouth, and I fall to the floor. My lip pulsates with pain, and I taste something metallic in my mouth.

"Oh, that's going to cost you some negative points," Mark says.

Before I can regain my composure, my head is yanked back by the hair. Mark forces me on my feet and throws me toward the kitchen. The counter stops my momentum when I slam my stomach against it.

"You stupid, ungrateful bitch," Mark says.

162

I hear him approaching me. My eyes scan the counter, and I see the heavy pan I used to make spaghetti. Mark's hand firmly grabs my shoulder, but my fingers have already grasped the handle of the pan.

He spins me around, and that gives me extra momentum when I swing the pan. I close my eyes and hear a hollow *bonk* come from Mark's face, followed by a yowl.

When I open my eyes, Mark's hand is no longer on my shoulder, and he's on the floor, raising his hand to his nose. Blood pours out of his nostrils and down his mouth. I can see that his nose is slightly crooked. I would have felt immense satisfaction if it weren't for what happens next.

"You slut!" Mark hisses.

I can see that one of his front teeth is chipped, too.

He's furious. Whatever he wanted to do to me ten seconds ago, it'll be much worse now.

I drop the pan and run around the counter. I know what he's about to do to me is really bad, but all I can think is: He can be hurt!

This entire time, I considered him to be untouchable, but that's not the case. He's not a god like he tried to lead me to believe. He's a human being, like me.

Mark's hand reaches across the counter. The tips of his fingers grab the hem of my shirt, but I manage to pull away. I run to the window, grab the fake plant, and turn to face Mark.

He's made his way around the counter and is walking toward me.

Without thinking, I hurl the pot at him. Bits of dirt scatter as the object flies through the air. Mark puts his hand in front of himself and effortlessly deflects the pot.

I look around for anything else to use. Not only do I have no weapons in sight, but I'm also trapped inside the living room.

"Come here!" Mark says.

I run around the coffee table, but Mark easily manages to grab a clump of my hair and pull me toward him. His arm headlocks me, pressing down on my throat.

"So, this is how it's going to be, huh?" he hisses in my ear. "Oh, you're so going to regret doing that."

"Please, let me go," I say.

Tears are running down my cheeks. I'm not struggling anymore because I know it will only make things worse, but my eyes are fervently scanning the room for any weapons I can use.

"You have no idea what trouble you just put yourself into, you ungrateful bitch," Mark says.

He drags me toward the kitchen table and grabs the remaining fork off it. He brings it to my cheek, way too close to my eye.

"I'm going to cut your eye out, and then you are going to pull four of your teeth out with pliers. And that's only going to be the start of your punishment," he says.

"Mark, please!" I cry.

I know deep down that begging him to let me go will make no difference, but I can't help it. I'm too scared for my own safety.

"Shut up! Or I'll take both your eyes!" he shouts.

I press my lips tightly and force myself to go quiet. I whimper with a closed mouth.

It's over. He has won. The best thing I can do is take the punishment he has concocted for me because resisting will only make things worse.

164

The tines of the fork are sliding up my cheek and inching toward my eye. I've instinctively squeezed my eyes shut, but the tears won't stop pouring out.

It doesn't matter how much I cry. It won't change anything.

"You did this to yourself, Amy," Mark says, and his timbre is soft again.

I can tell he's taking great pleasure in this.

Just then, the doorbell rings.

Both Mark and I freeze. The fork is no longer on my face.

Please, whoever you are, save me. Please, please, please.

"Who the hell is that?" Mark tightens the lock on my neck. "Did you call someone?!"

I can't speak because my throat is being crushed, so I shake my head.

"Police! Open up!" a muffled voice shouts on the other side.

"You called the cops?!" Mark asks.

The fork is now pressed under my chin.

I didn't! I try to say, but he won't let go of my neck.

I hear a bang on the door. Then another, and I hear something cracking at the frame.

Mark's lock on my neck releases. He grabs me by the wrist and raises my hand. He puts the fork in my hand and pushes me on the floor. I instinctively hold the fork tightly in my hand.

The door bursts open, and figures pour inside. A group of police officers is pointing their guns in the general direction of me and Mark.

"Officers! Thank God you came here when you did!" Mark says. "She tried to stab me with a fork!"

I look up at Mark and see that he has now changed completely. His body has somehow shrunk to portray *victim* body language. His eyes are wide in terror as he's pointing at me. The blood on his face makes him look even more like a victim.

The officer closest to me looks down at me. I can see his eyes flitting to the fork in my hand.

I instinctively raise my hands and drop the fork as I shake my head, but I can't find the words.

But the police officers don't seem interested in me in the slightest. Their guns are raised toward Mark, and one of them shouts, "Put your hands where I can see them! Right now!"

Mark tries to reason with them, "Officers, you don't understand! She's the one who attacked me! She—"

The officers' shouting drowns out Mark's voice. They're commanding him to turn around and put his hands up.

"You don't understand!" Mark shouts.

"We understand very well, buddy. Now, do us a solid and turn around. Slowly," one of the officers says.

They've already decided that Mark is the perpetrator. How? I have no idea. I'm just happy not to have the barrels of those guns pointed at me.

Mark is back to his old self again—the *victim* body language is gone, the terror in his eyes, too. He's ogling the police officers with an angry expression. Then, his eyes fall on me.

I have never seen such unfiltered hatred in someone's eyes before.

"Don't do it!" one of the officers shouts.

But Mark isn't listening. He's already lunging at me. He knows it's over, but he isn't going to give up until I'm dead, just like Adrienne, Mary, and Faith.

He doesn't like to lose.

Unfortunately for him, things in life don't always work out the way we hope they would. The moment Mark takes a single step toward me, the apartment is filled with deafening gunshots.

I instinctively put my hands over my ears and squeeze my eyes shut. The explosions seem to last forever. I don't even realize they're over until I feel someone gently touching my shoulder.

I scream and recoil as the police officer tries to calm me down. He and his coworkers need a few minutes to get me to stop screaming. By then, I'm on my feet, and they're escorting me out of the apartment.

My shocked mind only then remembers Mark, and I swivel to look for him. He's face-down on the floor, his head turned away from me, motionless. I can see red holes in his back and blood on the floor, and I don't need to stare too long in order to understand he's dead.

The next few minutes are a blur. I remember being escorted out of the building, seeing flashing blue and red lights, and being taken to the ambulance vehicle for treatment. I remember being given hot chocolate and a blanket, and I remember the paramedics checking to make sure I wasn't hurt.

What I remember clearly, though, is a woman shouting my name, running toward me, and embracing me in such a tight hug that I almost recoil because the grip reminds me of Mark so much. It takes me a moment to realize it's

Catherine. I hug her back even tighter, and we both cry uncontrollably.

One Week Later...

"It was you all along?" I ask Catherine.

We're sitting at my old apartment and sharing mint chocolate ice cream from the tub. The landlord was nice enough to let me back in because of what happened to me. I guess he doesn't care since he has a dozen other apartments that he's leasing.

"Yes, I'm the one who called the cops," Catherine says.

Her phone rings. It rang at least three times in the past hour. Ever since Catherine published her story about Mark and his victims, she's become something of a mini-celebrity.

"Another unknown number," she says as she declines the call and puts the phone into her pocket.

"Wait, I'm really confused. Sorry, my head is still messed up because of everything that happened," I say. "So, you called the cops to rescue me?"

"Yes."

"But why? I mean, after that... evidence you found of me and Rick doing stuff behind your back..."

"I knew that was a lie," Catherine says.

"What? How?"

I scoop up the softest part of the ice cream and raise it to my mouth, but I pause.

"Because I made it up," Catherine says.

I almost drop the spoon.

"You made it up? Cat, why?"

I don't have the capacity to be angry at her because she saved my life by calling the cops. Before coming to visit me today, she had told me she would tell me the full story. I'm willing to listen to the whole thing before I decide if a tantrum is justifiable or not.

"Let me take it from the top. It'll be easier that way," Catherine says.

She stabs her spoon in the hard part of the ice and shifts on the couch so that she's facing me.

"Adrienne Mendoza was my sister," she says.

This time, I do drop the spoon into the tub. The ice cream is invisible to me in that moment.

"Your sister?" I ask.

"Half-sister, to be precise."

"That's why you don't share the same last name?"

"Yes."

"Oh, Catherine. I'm so sorry." I put my hand over hers.

She flashes me a somber smile. "Adrienne had dated Mark for about a year or so before committing suicide. I hadn't known about Mark back then. I knew she had a boyfriend, but none of us knew anything about him. We never suspected he might have been the perpetrator."

"I see." I pick up the spoon, but I'm not digging for ice cream anymore. I'm just fiddling with it.

"Everyone forgot about it and came to terms with the fact that Adrienne might have had issues that she didn't tell any of us. But I couldn't let it go, so I started digging. And the more I dug, the less everything made sense."

"That's when you found out about Mark?"

"No. It wasn't until the third victim that I managed to put the dots together and figure out that all three girls had dated Mark at some point."

"Why didn't you go to the police?"

"I didn't have enough evidence. I had reasonable suspicion to believe he was involved, but that was it, I'm afraid."

I'm sitting in a way that I'm facing Catherine. I don't know when I have shifted, but I'm so focused on Catherine's story that I don't pay attention to it.

"You never told me about Adrienne. It must have been hard losing her," I say.

"I didn't want to reveal any details because I was afraid they could jeopardize the case," Catherine says.

"I guess you were right to do so. I can't imagine what would have happened if I had accidentally told Mark about you having a sister named Adrienne."

"Right."

Catherine pulls the spoon out of the ice cream mound and licks it.

"So, wait a second. I have a question," I say. "When we went to Kayla's party..."

"I had a feeling Mark was gonna be there," Catherine interrupts. "It was a long shot, but he had been looking for a new victim after Faith Barnaby, and he just so happened to be friends with one of Kayla's friends."

"That's how he found out about the party, right?"

"Yeah."

For about ten seconds, we remain silent as we eat ice cream. I'm eating too fast because of the adrenaline surging through me, and my teeth hurt.

"So, was it your plan all along to have me hook up with Mark?" I ask.

"No. The plan was for *me* to hook up with him." Catherine laughs. "But he worked fast. Not even ten minutes in and he was already on you. I knew it was too late for me to get involved then."

"So you played along, but you knew who he was?" I ask.

"Yes. And I had to think of something before my plan went to hell."

"So, you lied about the whole me and Rick thing?"

"Yes."

"You are a psychopath."

We both laugh at that. I don't really mean what I said. Sure, Cat may be a manipulator, but she never uses that to hurt other people.

"So, are you and Rick still a thing, or...?" I ask.

"God, no. We never were a thing to begin with." Catherine scoffs. "That's just a lie I had to make up to do what I needed to for the case."

"But you danced with him."

"And he's a terrible dancer."

"That still doesn't explain how you knew I was in trouble," I retort.

Catherine smiles. "Remember that time I came by Mark's place to give you your things?"

"Yes."

Catherine doesn't continue explaining. She waits for realization to hit me in the face.

And it does. It hits me so hard I want to facepalm myself for not realizing it sooner.

"The teddy bear. There was a camera in it, right?" I ask.

"It was another long shot," Catherine says. "I knew by then how Mark functioned. I knew he'd want to rub it in your face that you no longer had your best friend. I had hoped he would place the toy somewhere visible."

"And he did."

"And he did."

More silence.

"But what if he hadn't?" I ask.

Catherine gives me a look. "Amy, please. I always have a plan B."

I let out a chuckle of relief.

"I can't believe how elaborate your whole plan was," I say.

"Well, I'd been working on that case for years. And I still had a few slip-ups."

"Speaking of which, won't you get into any legal trouble for putting a camera inside Mark's apartment?"

"Already solved. Mark was a very dangerous individual, so the judge recognizes that the illegality of what I did can be waived because of the danger of the case itself."

Catherine's phone rings again. She groans as she reaches into her pocket and mutes it.

"There. Can't get a moment of peace these days," she says.

"Well, you are a hero after all."

"And you're a survivor. Imagine what kind of a book we could publish together."

I reach into the tub to get more ice cream, but Catherine puts a hand on my wrist. When I look up at her, her eyes are glistening with tears.

"I'm so sorry for letting you go through all of that," she says with a breaking voice.

"Cat, what are you talking about? You saved me from Mark. Who knows how many more girls you've saved."

"I know, but I know your life with him was a nightmare."

"Hey, if it stops scum like him from hurting another person, then it was all worth it. Besides, some good came out of it."

My company has rehired me after the story of Mark went public. I knew they just wanted to have the face of a survivor in their company for better publicity, so I was able to negotiate a good promotion. I now have my own office.

"Just fill me in on the details next time so I can help you take your target down."

Catherine smiles. "I'm glad you say that because I'm already working on another case, and I need help. I can't think of a better partner. What do you say? You in?"

I think about all the girls who might go through the same trauma as me. I remember how helpless I had been and how helpless they might be.

Adrienne Mendoza. Mary Campbell. Faith Barnaby.

I don't need time to think about my answer. I'm more than ready to take down another target like Mark.

"Hell yeah, I'm in," I say.

THE END

MORE BOOKS IN THE SERIES

1. Not My Husband
2. Never Leave Me
3. Inside These Walls
4. The House Across The Street
5. Mother Knows Best
6. Feel Free To Scream
7. Maria

Manufactured by Amazon.ca
Bolton, ON

45564551R00102